His

Quickly, you strip me out of my clothes. Then you lift me and set me down on our large dining room table. I feel the slick surface of the old-fashioned cherry-printed oilcloth, and I wonder why that rubbery sensation is making me wet. With a wink, you reach for our handcuffs (stashed under your chair) and bind my wrists. Then you tell me to wait, that you'll be right back. So I wait, cuffed there, growing wetter by the second. I'm making a little puddle beneath me, but I can't help that. There's nothing I can do about being so damn excited....

His

30 Erotic Tales Written Just for Him

by Alison Tyler & Thomas Roche

with a foreword by Barbara Pizio,
Executive Editor, *Penthouse Variations*

Books published by
Pretty Things Press
contain sexual fantasies.
In real life, make sure you practice safe sex.

His

Cover Design: Eliza Castle

First Pretty Things Press Edition 2003

First Printing January 2003

ISBN 1-57612-186-0

Manufactured in the United States of America
Published by Pretty Things Press

987654321

Water, water I desire,
Here's a house of flesh on fire...

—Robert Herrick

Dedicated to Tracy—
TS

Dedicated to SAM—
AT

Contents

Foreword

There is nothing more deliciously indulgent than erotic fantasy—those private moments when you can visualize your most extravagant dreams or savor sensual moments from your past. Fantasy can heighten the already luscious thrill of anticipation, letting you envision the endless carnal possibilities hidden within every sexual encounter. It can take you to places that exist only in your mind, allowing you to be whoever and do whatever you choose with an inconceivable array of partners. The lustful dreams that flutter through your imagination offer the tempting opportunity to shape them to suit your every erotic whim, creating a custom fit for whatever your heart desires.

Some of the fantasies you'll read in this collection are welcomingly familiar, while others will lead you to places that you'd least expect. You'll discover the myriad of pleasures that await when a friend confesses her secret longings and experience the thrill of a long-time lover revealing her sexiest dreams. You'll have passionate encounters with alluring strangers in unusual settings, but also discover adventure in the comfort of familiar surroundings. You'll find yourself in the middle of risque late-night threesomes with sensual women who aim to please—and who don't give a second thought to the time or place, seizing erotic opportunity wherever they can find it. You'll revel in the decadence of illicit affairs, enjoying each forbidden moment. You'll have furtive conversations with clandestine lovers, which will show you that words can sometimes be as stimulating as actions.

Within these pages, you'll also uncover provocative stories which dare to push boundaries, because in the anything-goes setting of your deepest fantasies, the world truly is your sexual playground. Feel free to explore a new kink or two. Visit a sex club and enjoy the charms of lovers new and old. Dabble in some erotic spanking and show her how good it feels to be bad. Switch roles for the night and allow her to explore her masculine side. Let go of your inhibitions and submit to her erotic demands. All of these delectable opportunities are spread out before you like a sensual banquet. The choice is yours to make.

The women telling these tales are woman you've met. You've passed them by in bars and clubs, shopping malls and downtown cafes. Don't let their looks deceive you. Whether they seem to be boldly searching for sexual adventure or appear innocent and sweet, an erotic fantasy land is swirling inside their minds, just waiting for you to discover. The naughty words that fall from their lipstick-slick lips are matched only by how daringly they live out their fantasies. This collection is made up of just a few of their tantalizing stories.

So let their sensuous voices whisper in your ear. Be seduced by their sexy words and dreams. Let their fantasies become yours.

—Barbara Pizio
Executive Editor, *Penthouse Variations*

Every Friday Night...

You watch me and my girlfriend dancing together. The music is loud and hard, and the drummer has worked himself into a lather pounding on the finely stretched skins of his expensive set. Most of the other patrons in this rocking club are dancing just as fast as we are. Swirls of vibrant color catch my eye as the dancers move together—scorching blurs of vamp red and glistening gold and unforgiving black. But you sit quietly at a booth in the corner, and you slowly drink your imported beer from the bottle and watch.

I catch on long before Shelly does. I see your eyes widen when I slip one arm around her slim waist and pull her closer to me. She responds automatically by gliding her sweet hips against mine in an almost accidental caress. The heat of her body makes me tremble, even though we always dance like that, delighting the guys wherever we go. The music turns us on—that rock 'n roll beat makes us think of something far more sexy than dancing—but knowing that men are watching our every move turns us on even more. Shelly's such a fair blonde and she perfectly compliments my dark hair, dark eyes. We fit together. Body to body. Skin to skin.

Tonight, Shelly's wearing a dark purple dress with a halter-style top. The thin satin ribbons tie together under her wave of long blonde hair and then trail loosely down her naked back. Her skin is sun-glazed, bronze and shimmering from the glitter she dusted on before we left her apartment. I tease her by tripping my fingertips dangerously along the tie at the back, as if I'm going to release the bow that will unveil her beautiful body. One pull and all will be revealed.

At my touch, she glances over her shoulder at me, locking onto my expression, and the look in her startling blue eyes says, "Naughty girl—"

When I peek over my shoulder at you, I see the same vision echoed back at me in your eyes. Yes, I'm a naughty girl. I'd have to be to dance this way with my girlfriend. To dance in public as if I wanted to spread her out on the floor and fuck her.

From your fixed gaze, I know exactly what you're thinking. You'd like to slide your lean body right between ours and see how you'd fit. Shelly behind you, tapping her fingers along your strong back, me in the front, kissing my way down the flat plane of your chest before moving down lower, opening up my mouth and taking your cock within. My lips are berry-slicked tonight, shiny with a sticky gloss called Triple-X. Yes, I bought it for the name. I can picture leaving kiss-shaped imprints on your bare skin as I worked. I like to be able to look at the road map of pleasure afterward, to touch each kiss with my fingertips before starting along that route again.

I'm getting turned on thinking about going down on you. I know how much you'd like me to lick up and down the length of your rigid rod, using the very tip of my tongue, darting it between your legs to touch your balls with a kitten-like stroke. Then moving back up and using the whole of my mouth. Sucking you in, drinking you down. I know how to work a man, to oblige obediently with my mouth. I never rush when I'm on my knees. There is something so fucking exciting to me about going down on a ready partner, about seeing how loud I can make a lover moan using only my lips and my tongue and my throat—

Shelly moves slightly now, to stand fully in front of me. She's lustfully eyeing the multi-tattooed bass player, and I take this opportunity to grab her and pull her back against me. Without a care of what someone might think, she firmly swivels her hips, her sublime ass now pressed firmly against the split of my body. I breathe in and catch the scent of her perfume. I know the name—was with her at the high-end Beverly Hills' department store when she bought it—but now, I'm thinking about the way she smells out at the beach, drenched in a combination of tropical suntan oil and the sweet sheen of dewy sweat from a hot day spent baking beneath the Santa Monica sun. And I'm thinking of the way she would look spread out on my bed, with you pumping over her. White sheets crumpling. Bodies merged together.

"He's watching," I whisper, leaning in to press my lips against the nape of her neck. "Shell, he's watching—"

She half-turns to glance over her shoulder, locates you quickly, and then gives you a sexy smile, batting her mascara-rich eyelashes in a silently sensuous invitation. That's the only encouragement you need. The band heats up, pressing onward. Without a need to rush, you calmly set down your beer and make your way through the crowd. Just as slowly, I release Shelly and let you slip between us. My arms go naturally around your waist, and I hold you close. So excited, I press the side of my face against your black shirt and feel the warmth from your body. We're not dancing to the music anymore—at least, not to the music that the rest of the patrons hear. This is a uniquely serpentine samba, a trio of heat, pressed together on the black-and-white checkered floor.

I wish that we were alone and naked, and then I wish that we were right here and naked, with an audience watching us fuck. Every move, every thrust, would be witnessed by a crowd of hungry onlookers. You'd take turns working the two of us, but you wouldn't play favorites. First, you'd dip your rigid cock into Shelly's pussy, then slide over and drive inside me with your pole all glossy from her juices. I think you'd know instinctively that I like a harder ride than

Shelly does. When you got to me, you'd give me everything you had, saving the sweeter tastes for my friend. I like to really feel it. When I'm fucking, I want to know that fact with every part of my being. I try to tell you that by the way that I'm dancing against you. I try to send you silent messages.

When the musicians take a break between sets, the three of us do, too, walking quickly to the exit and then out into the balmy Hollywood night. The summer heat wave gives the dark night air a fantasy feeling, as if we're on vacation on some paradise island, a place where anything goes.

Shelly's in the lead, and you and I follow a pace behind, watching her. She's got a high-class ass, and she twitches it when she walks, moving exaggeratedly as she stalks along the sidewalk in her racy spike heels. Because Shelly knows we're watching, she puts an extra shimmy in her step just for show, making me giggle at her total lack of discretion.

Your warm fingers entwine with mine, and you bring my hand to the fly of your jeans, so I can tell that your cock is hard and ready. I feel as if my legs will give out. You're so hard I don't know if I can wait. I want to drop to my knees right here on the cracked sidewalk, open my mouth and suck you until your cock hammers against the back of my throat. I don't care about laddering my stockings, don't care about getting dirty. When I make a little whimpering sigh to let you know my urgency, you give me a stern look, then shake your head. "Patience," you murmur to me, your first word of the evening, and I swallow hard and try to wait my turn.

I brought the pickup tonight, and Shelly gets to the truck bed first, climbs over and laughs when she sees the mattress roll in the corner. I've come fully prepared to make this erotic event as comfortable as possible. Shelly undoes the buckles and spreads out our makeshift bed, and the three of us camp out on it together. There are stars above and gold lights dance in the heavens, heralding distant clubs.

You wait in the center of the mattress as Shelly and I each take a side. The three of us stare upward as if in silent meditation, but our hands are already busy, pulling open buttons, undoing zippers, kicking off shoes, losing stockings and garters. There are hands helping me—your hands, Shelly's. I know her fingernails are painted a dark, rich blue that sheens like neon. I know she wears a silver ring around the middle finger of her left hand. Her touch is light, but not tentative. Your hands are different. Rougher, worn. You move without any hesitation, pulling on the mouth of the zipper that runs the full length of my slinky black dress. I shudder as the silver metal teeth give way and I am suddenly naked, my dress spread out and open around me.

Shelly leans over you to get to me, and you give a dark moan as her naked breasts brush your lips. As Shelly kisses me, you open your mouth and tease the undersides of her bouncing breasts with the tip of your tongue. Her lips on mine are warm and soft. I reach to grip into her heavy hair, sealing her to me as I lunge into her kiss. The pleasure is instantaneous, spiraling me onward with the promise of what lies ahead. But I'm yearning for more. And now I can't keep quiet about it. "I need—" I say, and that's all it takes, the magic word that unlocks the gates of our pleasure.

Then the three of us are naked and in motion. I climb on top of you, straddling your glorious body, slipping up and then down again as I fall into just the right rhythm. Shelly's using your mouth, her hands under her breasts as she dips one rosy pink nipple and then the other between your willing, parted lips. We're off in the corner of the parking lot, but it's not as if we have any semblance of privacy. This is Los Angeles, after all, and even at this late hour, couples make their way in and out of clubs and restaurants all along the strip. I like the fact that anyone could see us if they wanted to, if they turned their heads in our directions. I've always liked being on display, even if it's only for the gigantic sunglass-shaded eyes of a billboard of Angelyne on the building above.

As I ride you harder, Shelly moves down between your legs, and I can tell the exact moment she starts to lick your balls. Your expression changes. The look in your eyes hardens into stone for a moment, then seems to melt. I imagine what Shelly's warm tongue must feel like against your balls. Her fine hair tickles my skin as she works you more seriously. The sound of your breathing catches suddenly, and as I pump up again on my thighs, I can tell that you're about to come. We're a sliver of space away from that moment of release.

I lean forward, gaining the connection I need against your body, and my clit responds immediately to the sensation. When you slam into me, you lift me upward toward the sky, and for a moment I feel as if I'm flying. I want to keep riding you, keep pumping to reach my limits, but as soon as you come, Shelly is on me, pulling me from you and spreading me on the mattress. It's her turn. She wants attention now, and she knows the best way to get it. We hit the sixty-nine in tune and turned on. I work Shelly without thinking, lost in the feeling of pleasure from her hot mouth on my cunt.

Her lipstick smears against my skin. I feel that oily moisture on my most tender lips, and then I feel her mouth pursed as she so gently nips around my clit. She wants the two of us to come together. I sense this without her ever saying a word. And I know that she needs more to catch up to me, which is why she's working me slowly. I have to disengage myself from my own wants. My selfish desire is to press hard against her mouth and take what I need. But that wouldn't be fair. So I focus on what Shelly needs, and I give it to her, licking and sucking, making the types of maze-like tracings she craves when she's dying to come. Losing myself in the scent of her, in the world between her legs.

I hear you when you start to jack off, unable to stop yourself while watching the two of us play together like randy cats in heat. I know you're going to come on Shelly's back as she comes on my tongue, and that's the image that takes me over the top. The mess of it all. The thought that I will be able to reach out and trace my fingers through the thick honey-like liquid of your spent pleasure. When you rain down on Shelly's naked skin, she sighs and grinds herself against my mouth, so hot, so desperate. Her sweet moans reverberate against my naked pussy, and I reach that place one second after her, a tangle of limbs, a mess of sex.

The three of us are so sticky afterward. Just sticky and silent for a moment as we fumble with clothes in the back of the truck. And then we sprawl out again, incorrectly buttoned and under-dressed. We're packed close together, looking up at the midnight sky. "Tonight was amazing," you say, holding us close to your body. "My two sweet girls."

"It was almost as if you really didn't know us—" I tease, and Shelly laughs her musical laugh and rolls over to give you a hug. Because, you know, you say the same thing. . . every Friday night.

One on One

You're across from me on the couch, and it turns me on more than I could have imagined. It turns me on because you're watching me.

I'm wearing that short little dress, the one you like so much. One leg is up on the back of the couch; the other is on the floor. I'm not wearing any panties, and my hand is underneath, between my spread legs.

I'm slowly stroking my pussy. I'm very, very wet, just from having you watch me. My toys are laid out on the coffee table next to me: every now and then, I see your eyes flicker to them with anticipation, with excitement. I can't believe I'm being such a dirty girl, letting you watch me. I can't believe it, but I love it.

I pull the skirt up higher, tucking it so my pussy remains fully exposed. I don't think you noticed until now that I shaved for you. You look a little surprised, and that turns me on even more. Did you think I wouldn't remember the conversation we had a while back about how sexy a shaved pussy is to you? And it seemed like the perfect time, since I wanted to make sure you could see *everything*.

I start with two fingers—usually I go for one at the beginning, but I'm much, much too turned on to settle for just one finger. Your eyes go wide as you watch them slide in. I'm moaning softly, squirming on the couch, my body moving in time with the throb of techno music from the stereo. I work my two fingers in and rub my clit with my thumb. My clit is hard, very hard, and it feels so good to stroke it. Watching you has me so turned on that I could probably come almost right away. But I don't want to come just yet; I want to savor your eyes on me, just like everything else I do when I'm alone.

I take the vibrator, press the tennis-ball-sized head against my clit. I gasp as my pussy clenches around my fingers. My eyes shut for a moment as I see stars; when I open them, I see you've got your cock in your hand, slowly stroking it as you watch me. It's like we're in a peepshow booth, me putting on a show for you—and maybe you for me, too. That thought turns me on even more, and it makes me slip my fingers out of my pussy and reach for more toys.

I start with the narrowest of the three dildos. It slides inside me beautifully; I'm so wet that at first I don't even need any lube. I press the vibrator harder against my clit, arching my back as I gasp in pleasure. You're stroking faster, now, more and more turned on as you sense me getting closer. Holding eye contact with you as you stroke your cock, I reach out to the table again.

I ignore the middle-sized dildo and pick up the largest, putting the vibrator down across my lower belly just long enough to dribble lube on the tip of the dildo. Then I slide the silicone cock inside me, and the thickness of the head feels so good inside me I think, for a moment, that I'm going to come. But I don't; I just hover there, so close, as I watch your hand moving up and down on your hardness. God, I want you to come before I do. I don't know why; I just want to see your cock spurt, hear your moans of pleasure before I let myself go. I want to come knowing that my self-pleasure got you off, too, knowing that my fucking myself was enough to send you over the edge.

"Come for me," I say to you.

"Fuck your pussy," you sigh, and it's music to my ears. I begin working the thick dildo in and out of my pussy, holding the head of the vibrator firmly against my clit as I do. Your hand pumps furiously and I recognize that sense of urgency that happens just before you come. I have to back off on the vibrator, taking it all the way off of my clit, because you turn me on so much I think I'm going to come. But all of a sudden I know it's going to happen. The way your body twists, the way your hand tightens. And then you cry out, and come shoots out onto your hand.

The rush overwhelms me. I push the vibrator against my clit and move the dildo in and out of me rapidly, and I'm coming almost before you're finished. I thrash back and forth on the sofa, you coaxing me on with your moans of pleasure as you stroke your softening cock. My orgasm envelops me and I soar into it, my whole body alive with pleasure as our eyes meet.

My thighs come together, hard, and I have to turn off the vibrator or I'm going to start screaming. I relax into the sensations, feeling my pussy filled and my clit satisfied. I smile at you, as flirtatiously as I can manage, and I know I've fulfilled that fantasy you told me about. What I didn't expect is that you fulfilled mine.

And how convenient that is, since I'm planning to do it again. And again and again and again. One on one—just you and me.

A "Must Have"

"Really," my friend Kate said in her matter-of-fact tone of voice, "It's a no-brainer."

"What do you mean?"

"The cut is divine, and the color is absolutely perfect for you," she insisted, holding the negligee up to me. The racy lace-edged nightie of ice blue silk wasn't something I would have chosen for myself. Generally, I'm the type of girl who wears a simple tank-style T-shirt and cotton panties to bed. Yet at her insistence, I let Kate do the picking, and for the first time ever I started to understand her love of lingerie.

"Don't you like it?"

Although I was still dressed in my street clothes, the heat of the day had prescribed as little attire as possible. So on this balmy afternoon, all I had on was a skimpy white camisole top and a short rose-and-white checkered skirt. As she draped the nightie over me, the soft fabric rubbed against my skin, and I found the feeling intensely sensual.

"A must-have," she repeated, speaking to her reflection in the mirror. That's precisely when I saw you standing off to the left, almost out of the frame of the mirror's gaze. But I caught you looking at me, and you saw that I was looking back. Smiling slightly, you raised your eyebrows up in a silent question, and I nodded slowly in response. Yes, I said with that lift of my chin. Yes, definitely, yes. I would have agreed to anything, any query you asked me with your eyes.

"Good," Kate said, taking my head nod to mean that I'd decided on buying the thing. "Now, I'm going to find something for me. I deserve a treat, as well." Oblivious of the fact that I was staring at you, off she went, while you moved even closer. What were you doing in the lady's area? I couldn't wait to find out.

"Lovely," you said softly, and I looked at the nightie in my hand and once again I nodded.

"Not that," you continued. "You."

I wanted to say something clever, to respond in a cool and calm way, but unfortunately that's not my style. Kate is world's better at the quick-talking banter. She knows how to flirt, how to tease with her words and with her sexy, double-entendre expressions. When we go out drinking together, Kate rules the bar, while I'm all about shy smiles and glances from under my long dark lashes.

To give myself time, I primped in the mirror, still holding the nightie in my hand, and I felt myself growing excited. The way you were looking at me. The fact that we were strangers caught in the middle of the sexiest place in the store, a corner filled with a rainbow of thongs and imported bras and whale-boned corsets. Finally, I knew what to do.

"It's hard—" I paused, grinning when your eyes opened wider, "hard to decide without seeing it on." I glanced behind me to the door to the dressing rooms, and that was all you needed. Without a word, you led the way. Quickly, before anyone would notice, we hurried down the hallway together. I was certain we hadn't been spotted. The only people in the section were Kate, off in a corner, talking bras with the saleslady, and a middle-aged woman manhandling the girdles. That was it. Who shops for lingerie in the middle of a Monday afternoon? Two single girls playing hooky from the most boring sales conference in the world—and you. What were you doing there, pawing through the bras and panties? Buying something for some special someone? Or did you catch my eye as you walked past, and made it your business to find out something more about me?

Didn't really matter, did it? What mattered was the fact that we had to find a room to share—and fast.

We hurried to the large dressing room at the very back, and you sat down on the seat and waited for me to change. And I did change. Inside, I changed as I peeled out of my light, summer-weight clothes, some part of me disbelieving that I was actually doing this: stripping for a stranger. The thought pleased me immensely and aroused me even more. Moving with exaggerated slowness, I pulled my shirt over my head, revealing the fact that I was braless underneath the thin lycra, that my breasts were free of any hindrance. Then I slipped off my shoes, unzipped my skirt and let it fall to the floor in a ripple of checkered fabric. With a small smile on my lips, I stood before you, nearly nude, waiting for you to hand me the lingerie.

You didn't.

Instead, you came to stand behind me, so that we could see ourselves reflected in the mirror, once again. And you started to gently kiss the back of my neck, working your way lower and lower down my spine. Your hands were busy, roaming over my naked breasts, pinching my nipples, before moving down, to easily cup my pussy through my panties.

"I need to try it on," I reminded you.

Sighing at having to postpone our pleasure, you reached for the negligee and handed it over, and I slid the pretty finery over my head, trembling at the sensation of being caressed by silk. Now, I understood what Kate had been talking about. This was a completely different experience from wearing plan, old cotton. This was like slipping into a dream.

For a moment, you stared at me, as if I'd just transformed before your very eyes. Then you went on your knees on the dressing room floor and slowly slid my panties down from beneath the nightie. That was an amazing feeling, being dressed and undressed. My bare pussy gained contact with the smooth, cool silk for one moment before you hiked the slip-like creation up to my hips and pressed your mouth directly and firmly to my pussy.

Automatically, I brought my hands to your shoulders, needing to hold onto you to keep myself steady. Your mouth—oh, your mouth—the sweetness of it had me so fucking wet in a heartbeat. You worked me like an expert, the way you tickled my clit with the point of your tongue before kissing the lips of my pussy, pinching them together so that the moisture slid free. I looked up and saw myself in the mirror, and I almost couldn't recognize the woman reflected back at me. Who was this creature, this temptress, getting it on in a dressing room with a total stranger? A handsome stranger. An amazingly well-endowed stranger, I realized gratefully, as you moved to stand and unzip your fly, revealing your massive hard-on.

I wanted to feel your cock inside me more than I've wanted anything before. The urgency within me was like a primal scream. I mean, all I wanted to do was fuck you. But I needed to taste you first. My body told me what to do.

Open your mouth, my brain urged. *Open your mouth and take him in.*

Slipping onto my knees on the dressing room carpet, I took over your position, mouth open, and let you slide your cock within. I dragged my tongue along the length, delighting in the silky softness of your skin, the most beautiful-feeling skin against my tongue. I bathed you with the heat of my mouth, got your cock all wet with my open mouth, with the sucking motions. Bobbing my head up and down, I worked the length of you. But I was careful. I didn't want you to come, not without giving me exactly what I needed first. I wanted to make you feel as good as I possibly could, wanted to bring you right up to the edge, when your thoughts went hazy and confused, and you didn't know which way to go.

When I felt your hands stroking my hair, I moved. Without needing any instruction from you, I took my position—my favorite position—hands on the mirror. Body arched, I offered you the entry from behind. Doggy-style is such a sublime way to fuck. I like all parts of the position: the way a man can take charge while being behind, using his hands and his body against my own. You understood, and you took your spot and lifted the nightie from behind, then gripped my hips and entered me with one slow, long thrust.

If we'd been somewhere secluded, in your apartment or mine, I know that I would have screamed. I could hear the sound of the pleasure building in my head, the way I'd start out low, like a rumbling growl that would grow as you continued to fuck me. But I couldn't yell. Not without consequences. We were in public, after all. Even in our little private space, we were in public. So I lowered my head and shuddered, the silent scream reverberating inside of me instead. Bounding and rebounding off the walls of my body.

This was a necessary fuck. But until we began, I hadn't realized that it was something I desperately needed. Hadn't realized that it had been too long for my poor body. That I required pleasure the way I need food and shelter. Sure, I'm capable of stroking my own clit, of making myself come with my fingertips spiraling around and around, or with my vibrator revving on 'high,' but there's something different about being fucked by a lover. Something more satisfying about having an orgasm with a partner rather than solo-style. I guess that's why Kate had dragged me to the store in the first place, believing that if she could make me feel sexy with pretty frilly lingerie, I'd remember how important it was to connect with someone.

Now, I remembered. Your strong body moved against me. Your hands sought out the split between my legs, and your fingertips fluttered lightly over my clit, caressing gently at the perfect pace. You helped me along to the climax with your endlessly stroking fingertips, so that I could contract on your cock while coming. Raucously coming. Dramatically coming.

I saw my eyelids opening so wide, and then flutter until they were almost closed. I saw my lips part, although no noise came out. I just fell into it. Fell into the pleasure of the moment and the motion until we were coming together. You met my gaze in the mirror, locked onto me as you drove in so deep. I couldn't believe how connected I felt—staring into the eyes of a stranger while my body vibrated with the most delectable sensations of all time. That's how I felt when I came. So sweet. So perfect....

"So?" Kate asked when you and I exited the dressing room together. Her eyes were huge, focused first on the nightie balled in one of my hands, and then on you as you slid your business card into my other.

"A must-have," I said, grinning in your direction to let you know that I'd call.

Aisle Seat

I'm sitting in the departure lounge when I first see you. I try not to look at you, but I can't stop glancing up from my magazine as you get your seat assignment and sit opposite me, spreading out over several of the big, cushy chairs. You're incredible, so handsome in that dark, conservative suit with the bright blue shirt and red tie. When you take off your suit jacket and drape it over the seat next to you, I can see that the shirt fits tight and accents your broad shoulders. I don't realize how hard I'm staring at you, that I can't take my eyes off your body.

You fix me with your gaze and say "Hi." I glance back down to my magazine and smile a little, just the barest hint of flirtation in my gaze. I don't return your pleasantry, I just let you think what you want to think. But I'm lost in my own thoughts, and those thoughts are that I want you, just like that, immediately. I want to kiss you right here in the departure lounge, climb into your lap and kiss you, pull off your tie, open your shirt, rub my face against your body.

I'm reading an article in a women's magazine about how to give the perfect blow job, how to satisfy a man utterly. The photograph accompanying the story is a man's chest and stomach, a woman licking her way down his body with her mouth open wide. A faint treasure trail runs down between his six-pack abs. I read the description of how you should go down on your man, and I picture the pretty girl in the ad doing it to this incredible guy, to the cock that resides, quickly hardening, south of those perfect abs. Then I picture me doing that to you. My nipples stiffen in my business suit, pressing uncomfortably against my blouse, restrained by my lacy bra. I can feel an involuntary clench between my legs, and I know I'm getting wet.

I finish the article, close the magazine and stretch my arms. I smile at you again, and you smile back. I can tell you're looking at my breasts as I stretch, checking out the way the firm nipples show through my blouse. I want to be embarrassed, but I'm not. I'm flattered. I'm intrigued. I'm excited. I'm wet.

I look down demurely, look away to find the clock, check my watch, find any excuse to let my eyes flicker around the room to catch glimpses of you without letting you know I'm looking. I close my eyes and lean my head back, but I can see you from under my slitted lids, devouring my body. I think about the advice on blow jobs—prosaic stuff, really, barely even getting as far as deep-throating—but even the most elementary advice on sucking cock always makes me want to do it. I can't get the images out of my head, images of me going over to you, getting down on my knees, and putting all the techniques I've just learned into action.

I open the magazine again and find my place. The piece accompanying the blow job article is one on how to tempt him to go down on you. The photo for this one is the same couple, shot from the side, the woman's arms placed strategically across her breasts in a gesture of ecstasy while the man licks his way down her belly.

It's an incredibly suggestive photo, a little shocking to see it in a magazine like this one. It leaves nothing to the imagination. I know exactly what he's going to do to her; maybe the model even did that to her the second after they shot the photo. God, he's gorgeous. I picture his pretty face descending between her thighs, picture her model-perfect body twisting as his tongue finds her clit.

She's coming, hard, her hands pinching her nipples as

she arches her back and strains against him, pressing her clit harder onto his tongue. I glance up and see that you have full, beautiful lips and a well-formed chin with a five o'clock shadow. I can almost tangibly feel the faint stubble of your beard against my thighs as your face dips between my splayed thighs, feel the heat of your full lips against mine, your tongue caressing my clit.

You're still looking at me, aggressively, almost bordering on rudeness. I can tell you've taken special notice of my breasts, but as I cross my legs nervously, pressing my thighs tightly together, your eyes rove over them, as well. My skirt is a little shorter than I usually wear for business meetings, stopping a few inches above the knee. I'm used to drawing looks from men, but not men as attractive as you. Not men who make my stomach turn to Jell-O, my nipples grow firm and my pussy get hot and wet.

I've got to have you. I can't, I know, but I must. Funny how that works, sometimes.

They announce that boarding will begin in just a few minutes. I stand up and stretch, well aware that you're looking at me. I toss the magazine on the seat, well aware that I've left it open. I look at you and smile.

"Excuse me, Sir" I say. "Would you mind watching my bag? I'd like to go freshen up in the ladies' room before we board."

"Not at all," you say, your eyes flickering from my legs and breasts to my suitcase.

"Thanks," I say, and walk away, feeling your gaze on my butt, feeling you undressing me. What do you think I'm wearing under this conservative business suit? Something conservative?

I go into the ladies' room and find a stall. Pulling up my skirt, I can't resist a quick touch of my pussy, tugging the crotch of my thong out of the way. I knew I was wet, but I didn't realize I was *this* wet. Knowing it, now, turns me on even more. I pull the skimpy, off-white thong down my thighs, noticing how wet it is. Soaked through. I step out of it and tuck it in my pocket. I straighten my garters, make sure that my nude-colored stockings look right. I pull my skirt down and take a long time fixing my makeup in the bathroom mirror. I think the red lipstick is a little much, but I'm afraid you won't get the hint. I draw the line at eye shadow, though. I pull the pins out of my hair and let my hair down, fluffing it slightly.

"Thanks. I'm happy to return the favor," I tell you when I get back to the departure lounge.

"Nah, that's all right," you say. "They're about to board."

"No, really, I don't mind at all," I say firmly. "It's just around the corner. Go ahead."

What flashes through your mind at that instant? Surely that I'm a thief, one of those airport tricksters, that I'm going to run away with your laptop. But you nod, thank me, and head toward the rest room.

I glance around. Everyone is fumbling with their stuff, getting ready to stampede the line as soon as the flight attendants announce general boarding. Nobody is paying attention to what I'm doing, leaning over your jacket and quickly slipping something in your pocket.

When you return, you thank me again and I nod and rush over to the line. I don't want to be standing next to you while we board. Conversation might ruin this, might make me lose my nerve. In fact, I'm quite sure it will. All I want is for you to be gorgeous, breathtaking, mysterious.

By the time you get your jacket on, you're quite a ways behind me in line. I have to fight not to look right back at you, but I want to give you a few minutes. I suddenly remember, with horror, finding old half-eaten, melted candy bars and semi-molten chewing gum, ancient business cards from people I can't remember ever having met. Finding them in my suit jackets when I go to take them to the dry cleaners. But women have purses. Guys use their pockets more often, don't they?

I'm not sure, in general. But what I do know is that as I approach the gate, my ticket out, my suitcase towed like a child's wagon behind me, you're doing more than looking at me. You're doing more than undressing me with your eyes. And when I look down, I see that your hand is firmly stuffed in your jacket pocket.

I smile at you, bat my lashes, and lick my lipsticked lips.

You don't return the smile; if I were less experienced, I might think the look on your face was outrage. But it's not; I recognize it clearly, like the silhouette of a lover in the moonlight. It's lust, raw, pure, aching lust, and when I drop my eyes to your crotch I can see you shifting uncomfortably. I wink at you and turn around to hand the flight attendant my ticket.

You're seated several rows behind me, so I imagine that I can feel you looking at me, perhaps at the way my hair falls over the back of the chair, perhaps at the curve of my shoulder, the slope of my arm, which is probably about all you can see from where you're sitting.

We've both got aisle seats.

I glance through my magazine, taking note of the sex tips I already know, getting more and more turned on by the idea of putting them into practice. I'm quite sure you noticed where I left the magazine open to when I left it on my seat. Does that mean you think I'm a novice? Surely not. Though I guess I'm a novice at *this* sort of thing.

Sure, it's probably my imagination, but the effect it has on me is real. I can feel your impatience, feel you wondering when I'm going to make my move. I don't know if you're a gentleman; in fact, I have no idea. A gentleman would wait for me to choose the time. And you do—and I do. About an hour into the flight, when I'm squirming in my seat, I unbuckle, stand up, stretch, and take off my jacket. There's no line for the bathroom. I'm closer to the front of the plane, but I head toward the back. Passing you, I note your eyes on my body. I make eye contact. I know it's going to happen.

I slip into the bathroom and leave the door open. It's cramped in here; I put the seat down, sit, and wait.

My whole body feels alive and aching. I want you. When the door opens, my heart seizes in my chest; what if it's the flight attendant or some other passenger?

But it's you. You glance behind you to make sure no one's watching, then you come into the bathroom.

You look like you're about to speak, but I don't give you the chance. I lean forward, pushing you against the door as you fumble behind you to lock it. I'm on your belt in an instant, pulling it open, unhitching your wool pants, taking your zipper down as I look up into your eyes, enraptured by the naked lust I see there.

You're wearing boxers. I slip your cock out through the fly and take it in my mouth. Your cock tastes incredible—at once strange and familiar, salty with the dribble of pre-come I've squeezed out of the head. I swallow as much of it as I can and come up for air, letting my tongue laze around the swollen head as I caress your shaft with my hand. I feel your fingers running gently through my loose hair. Your faint moans are lost in the sound of the airplane engines and of rushing air. I let your cock out of my mouth and lick down the shaft, nuzzling your balls out of your shorts so I can lick them, too. Then I lick back up to the top and take you back into my mouth, easily swallowing all of you, feeling your thickness fill my throat.

Silently, as I suck you, I take stock of the space around me. By the time I stand up, I've already got the logistics worked out. I spread my legs and brace my knees on either side of the toilet, lifting my skirt. Are you surprised to find me wearing garters? Turned on, maybe? You already knew I wasn't wearing any panties, and I'm betting you figured out a way to sniff them, so it shouldn't be any surprise to you when you drop to your knees, push me forward, and dip your face between my thighs. It shouldn't surprise you to find me so incredibly wet.

Your tongue feels hot, and I can't suppress the moan that comes from my lips. Thankfully, we're in the rear compartment, close to the engines, atop the loudest noise in the plane. My gasps and faint groans are hidden in its roar. I grasp the sink and feel you press your tongue harder against my clit. I'm very close to coming, but I want to come with you inside me.

When I gently push you away, I have to squeeze tight against you to turn around. I pull my skirt up still higher, exposing my ass, and what happens next surprises me. Still kneeling behind me, you lean forward and take hold of my bare ass cheeks, part them gently, and let your tongue slide between them. I've never had that done to me before; my pulse races as I feel your tongue exploring my darkest spot. It makes my pussy throb as your tongue burrows between my cheeks. I'm afraid for just a split second it means you're going to expect to fuck me in the ass—and then I don't even care, I just want more. More of your tongue, delving into me where no tongue has ever been. I lean hard against the sink and spread my legs further, feeling the metal bulkheads bruising my knees.

You slide up my body, pushing me forward slightly, guiding your cock between my legs. I feel the head touch my lips, sliding up and down between them, feel it graze my clit. I gasp. Your cockhead finds my entrance and you penetrate me gently, feeling the head pop in as I push back onto you. The airplane swirls around me—have we hit a bout of turbulence, or is it just the feel of your cock driving deep inside me? I'll never know, because all I can feel right now is your flesh against mine, your cock entering me as deep as it can go. Silently, quite against my involuntary moans, you start to fuck me.

I have to stifle them as they rise in me. I have to bite my lip to keep from crying out. I'm so turned on I can't control myself. I can almost feel my knees bruising as I use them to shove me hard back onto you. You fuck me fast, like you're desperate to come, like our furtive fuck is going to come to an end any moment. But I'm so close, almost nothing could keep me from coming now, and when I reach down to touch my clit, it takes only the slightest of strokes before I explode around you, fighting to keep my moans to myself, my pussy clenching your shaft as you drive into me. I've barely finished coming when I sense you struggling with your own cries of pleasure, and then there's the hot pulse inside me as you let yourself go, come flooding my pussy.

Slumped forward against the sink, I look over my shoulder and see that same naked lust in your eyes.

You don't kiss me; you just look at me sternly as you tuck your cock, now slick with my juice and your come, back into your pants, as you zip up and buckle your belt.

Then you smile, the way you did out in the departure lounge, when you were first flirting with me. Your hand dips into your pocket and comes out holding my underwear.

"You'll need these, I think," you say.

"Probably not," I tell you, but I accept them.

After you've left, I take a moment to compose myself, to maintain the illusion that there's nothing out of the ordinary happening.

When I return to my seat, I don't look back at you. After the plane has landed, I risk a glance, and you meet my gaze unflinchingly. We smile at each other, then join the slow river of people heading out in the airport.

I lose sight of you in the labyrinth of aisles and corridors. It's not until I've hailed a cab and given him the address that I notice a crinkle in the pocket of my suit jacket.

I take out the piece of paper, unfold it.

It's a travel agent's itinerary. There's a passenger name, and a business address. And the details of a cross-country flight a week from today.

I notice that the itinerary already has a seat assignment.

You've requested an aisle seat.

Bedtime Story

I'll be honest, here. My roommate Justine was the one who wanted to hear you read. She circled your name in the paper, and when I whined about not wanting to go, she correctly pointed out that I'd dragged her to plenty events that bored her to tears.

"Please, don't make me," I said. "I'm tired."

Without listening to my lame excuse, she flat-out insisted that I accompany her to the bookstore down the street. "He's intense," she continued. "His words will make you melt."

"All right," I nodded. "Fine." But the possibility of melting was not the real reason why I accompanied her. I saw your publicity photo on the back jacket of the cover, and although I'm not the type to get star-struck, I was intensely intrigued.

Usually, the very concept of live fiction readings confuses me. The point behind them, that is. Why would anyone ever bother to attend? Short stories were meant to be read by one, in the privacy of one's own home. That's my opinion, anyway. Fiction isn't the same thing as a movie script—the words on the page were not intended to be dialogue for an actor to perform. Yet when Justine and I arrived at the store, the place was already packed. So I guess my opinion isn't a popular one. The customers in the audience thought that hearing you read would be a treat.

Justine and I found a spot at the back of the store, and we watched you approach the podium. And for a moment, the rest of the surroundings in the store faded from my awareness. I know there were children shrieking in the picture book nook, and I know that some rude driver outside was laying on the horn, but I saw only you.

The reading was sublime. You are a good writer, but more important for something like this, you are a good performer. Most authors lose themselves in their own work. They either mumble, or read too fast to get to some distant "good part," or seem so fucking proud of themselves that you can't help but hate them on sight. You were different. You held the audience with your subtle wit and your friendly banter, and when you read, there was as much hushed quiet from the crowd as you could hope for in a raucous place like a book store in the very heart of Berkeley. You finished to thunderous applause, and then a librarian-looking woman announced that you would be willing to sign any of your works.

Justine had a copy of your book already, and she joined the cue of people who wanted to own your name in ink. Still curious about you, I stood by Justine, pretending I was only there to keep her company. It took a long time to make it to the front of the line. When we arrived, you kindly signed Justine's copy, but I felt your eyes on me. I smiled at you, and horrified Justine when you asked if I had anything I wanted signed.

Don't know precisely what came over me. But just as if you were a rock star and I was some metal-minded groupie chick, I rolled up the sleeve of my delicate black crocheted sweater and offered you the tender inside skin of my wrist. You signed without a hesitation, and I crooned in a girlish giggle, "I'll never wash again!"

"That was fucking rude," Justine hissed as she dragged me away. "I can't believe you!"

"At least, I didn't bare my breasts," I told her. But then I looked down at my wrist and saw the name of the hotel and the room number, and when I looked over my shoulder, you were still staring at me.

It took every ounce of nerve for me to actually show up at your hotel in the city. I'm bold, as you must have guessed, but I'm not that bold. I didn't tell Justine I was going; I just said I had to leave, and then I headed for the bar at the hotel. It was an extremely fancy bar, at an extremely fancy hotel, and as I sipped my wine I tried to decide the ultimate question—should I stay or should I go? That's where you found me, sliding onto the stool at my side and putting your hand out to introduce yourself.

"I know who you are," I grinned, but I shook your hand anyway.

"But I don't know your name—"

I told you and you repeated it, as if liking the sound.

"I don't usually—" I started, brushing my hair quickly out of my eyes with my free hand.

"Neither do I," you said back, indicating your signature on my wrist.

"So what do we do, then?" I asked. "If we're two people who don't?"

"Maybe we could be two people who do—"

That was all it took. You put some money down for my drink and then we walked together to the bank of elevators. I was aware of how close we were standing to each other, and of how much closer I wanted to stand. When the elevator arrived, we waited impatiently while a party of six exited the space, and then we got on. I was surprised that we were all by ourselves. Surprised and, I must add, deeply pleased.

The elevator started to rise, and you quickly turned me so that I could see the view outside. The glass elevators at this high-end hotel are famous. From our vantage point, we could see the city of San Francisco, all bright lights and a collage of traffic down there growing smaller and more insignificant the higher we rose. I felt you pressing against me, your hard cock firm against my ass, and I sighed and closed my eyes. You must have been able to see my translucent reflection in the windows, because you said, "No, watch—"

At your words, I opened my eyes just as you slid your arms around me and bent to kiss my neck. Oh, did that feel good. Beyond good. Your warm mouth against my skin, the wetness of your mouth right at the perfect place. You sent shudders through my entire body with that single kiss alone. I saw the pleasure start to show in my face. Saw the violet glimmer in my eyes and the way my full breasts were lifted higher as I took in a deep breath. You slid my dress up in back and lowered my panties, then waited patiently for me to step out of them. The fabric of my dress fluttered against my bare skin, and I sighed at that extreme sensation—dressed but undressed. Inappropriately attired for public.

Then I felt your cock against me, pressing against the curve of my hip before sliding into me from behind. I put my palms flat on the glass windows as you thrust hard inside me. We were still in motion, riding all the way up and up and up—

The sound of the elevator's bell made us stop, and you quickly wrapped me in your embrace as the doors opened behind us. An older couple stepped in, and said a gracious hello as they pressed the button for their floor.

"Enjoying the view?" the woman asked, completely unaware that you were still inside me.

"Oh, yes—" I managed to reply.

"Which floor?" the man asked us.

"We're just on a ride," you said, and I giggled helplessly, knowing that your jacket covered the place where we were joined, but certain that if the woman looked at the reflection of my face in the window, she'd know precisely what we were doing. How could she not? Somehow, they remained oblivious, exiting on their floor, leaving us with words of goodnight. You reached around and hit the button for the top floor once more, and you fucked me during the ride. Fucked me so hard that I almost creamed right there. It was our own little room-witha-view. Moving room with a view. But when we arrived once again at the top floor, you slid my dress back into place and readjusted your slacks. Then we were out, hand-in-hand, walking to your suite.

Inside, we didn't make it to the bed. You pushed me up against the wall and took me like that. My legs wrapped around your waist. Your hands holding me steady. Lifting me up and then bringing me right back down on your steel-like rod.

I can't tell you how amazing that felt. The way you worked me. The way you played me. But what surprised me the most was the fact that we were silent. No words passed between us. Strange for a writer? I didn't know. I've never been with one before.

Afterwards, I asked you that nagging question. Why had there been no words?

"You like to talk?" you asked softly in the bed.

"I like to listen."

"A bedtime story, then?" you offered.

Now, I nodded, watching as you moved slowly down my body, positioning yourself at the split of my legs and starting to lick and lap between them. I was still liquified from our first round, but my body responded with ease, already ready for a second turn.

You made sweet circles with your tongue, and then you started to talk. The words didn't really matter. They reverberated against my most sensitive skin, and I gripped onto the sheets with both hands, tightening my body as you told me story after story of sex, and sweat, and heat, and sin. The most perfect bedtime story ever told.

Too Dirty To Clean

I'm not supposed to be calling you.

Maybe that's why I'm so damn wet. The concept of doing things I'm not supposed to turns me on. Crazy, but I didn't learn that simple, sinful fact until I met you. I lived my whole life up to this point believing that being good had its own rewards. I shook my head in dismay as I watched friends wander down the back alleys of life, and I judged them internally, smugly pleased with myself and how well I went about my own business with no soap opera dramas.

Now, I know better. From you, I've learned that bad girls truly do have all the fun. Which is fine, because I've crossed the line. I'm as bad as I can possibly imagine. This evening, my panties are sticky and clinging to me, and I am extremely aware of that dangerous heat and wetness at my center, and knowing that I will get no relief. Not tonight, anyway.

Because I'm *really* not supposed to be calling you. I'm supposed to be on my way to the corner grocery store, to pick up something I forgot today when I did the rest of the week's shopping. That was the excuse I gave, anyway. Lame though it may sound, it was all I could come up with through the hazy, horny fog of my X-rated thoughts. *Need tomato paste for the sauce. It won't taste as good without. So be right back, honey.* But "right back" isn't supposed to include a stop at a graffiti-tagged pay phone around the corner, where I slide in a silvery quarter, dial your number from memory, and tell you how much I miss you.

And how much I miss your cock.

"Say that again," you prompt.

"Cock," I repeat automatically. "I miss your cock—"

"Tell me more. What do you miss the most."

"I miss bending over, parting my thighs, and taking it."

"Taking what—"

"Your cock," I say again, and I hear the low chuckle caught at the back of my throat as some sane part of my inner critique witnesses me having this unbelievable conversation. I manage to shock myself with the words that come automatically to my lips when you and I are on the phone. Or in bed together. Or outdoors at some semi-secluded spot where we think we're safe. Where we think we're hidden—even though there is no real privacy in Los Angeles. Someone can always see you. That doesn't stop me from talking dirty. Because with you, I'm vulgar and I say things I wouldn't say in my other life. My real life. Where people think I'm good and kind and sweet and honest. With you, I say things that are darker, that cut closer to the bone. More importantly, I say things that are true. There's no need for false niceties, for faux conversational chatter. We don't have the inclination, and we don't have the time to fuck around. When we're together, we only have the time to fuck.

"Where are you?" you ask me now, and I know that you can hear the traffic sounds of La Brea, and I'm certain that you can picture how it must feel to be where I am—in *both* the mental and physical locations of where I am.

"You know—" I say.

"Tell me," the sadist in you insists. "Tell me, bad girl. Where are you?"

"Pay phone."

"Which pay phone."

"Down the street from our house."

"Our," you repeat caustically, to drive that point home. It's not *ours* as in yours and mine, it's ours as in mine and *his*. "Don't want to chance the number on your cell phone?"

I don't answer. I don't have to. Yet I understand perfectly well what you are doing. You want me to revel in it—the lies and the cheating, the sneaking out to make a simple phone call. If I'm going to do this, then you're making me do the wrong of it right. Every guilty moment. Every stolen embrace. You have nothing to lose, so you can play all the mental mind-fucking games you want. I have everything to lose, on some far distant level, but at times like this, I'm amazed to find that I don't care. I'd trade it all in at this moment to be with you, but when I say that, you pounce, already ready for me.

"Then why don't you call me from your place?" you tease, "or have me over for dinner?" and I imagine you in your bed, naked, one hand pumping your cock. You've told me before that you can come just to the sound of my voice. I don't have to talk dirty. I don't have to do anything except say words—any words—and your cock throbs. I could make you come by reading the telephone book aloud, by reading dictionary definitions, by reciting poetry in Latin. We have that kind of connection. The right one to have with the wrong guy. Or with the right guy, at the wrong time.

And you are the right guy. You are the one guy, the only guy, who has ever made me feel sexy in my own skin. Sexy when I walk across the room naked. Sexy when I push myself off of your sweaty body and look around the floor for my discarded clothes. I get wet when I think about you. I squirm in my jeans, and I feel the arousal start. Just by picturing your eyes when you look at me, when you don't have to tell me what you want, when I just know. Or the way you grab onto my hair when we fuck. Your fist wrapped around my ponytail, pulling hard. Hurting me. Making me arch my back and lift my chin, making me stare in the mirror over your bed and see myself. See what a cheat looks like. What a slut and a tramp and—

"How long have you got?" you ask.

"Not long enough to come over."

"But long enough to get me off—"

I've come while astride your cock. Pushing up to gain leverage and then sliding right back down to the base. That had never happened to me before—coming while fucking without any help. Without the added assistance of my hand or my partner's hand on my slippery clit, teasing and stroking. I thought I must be in love with you in order for that to have happened. But you saw what I was thinking and you just grinned at me and shook your head. We have that connection.

That white-hot fucking connection. When I see you, I just want to take off my clothes and bend over. Or lie down. Or straddle you. I want to suck you off, or spread my legs and let you lick in sweet circles around my clit. I want to pump my hand up and down your cock, jacking you off.

All I want to do is fuck you.

But it's not so simple. I don't know why or how I got to this point. This grown-up place where I'm supposed to do the right thing. What I know is that it's not easy. I never thought I'd be crossing the line that I've crossed with you. I never thought I'd relate to all those clever songs: *The Dark End of the Street. Slip Away.* Christ, even *Hurts So Good*. They're all about you and me. About what I want to do with you and what you're going to do with me.

"What are you wearing?" you ask next, and I look down, blushing at my lack of self-awareness, to see that I have no idea. I'm only thinking about you, and what you'd do to me if I could steal away tonight for long enough to let you. You'd be on me before I even shut your apartment door. You'd shred my clothes off me, push me up against the white plaster of your living room wall, and you'd fuck me so that I could feel it. Shaking me from the inside out. I'd grip into your skin, use my mouth to search for purchase on the strong ridge of your shoulder, bite you and mark you since you can't leave marks on me. I'd cry out loudly when I came. So loud and fiercely that it would sound as if I was in pain. Pleasure/pain. That's what it is.

I don't have it with him. He wouldn't pull my hair. He wouldn't slap my face or pinch my nipples until I cried out from that sharp spark of pain. He wouldn't put me over his lap and spank me, or push hard on my shoulders to make me kneel before him so that I could suck him off. Even if I asked, he wouldn't do those things to me. Instead, he'd get a disgusted look on his face and ask me where I could ever have come up with such a seedy idea. The same look I won from him when I suggested we check into a cheap motel sometime for a night of tawdry sex. The same expression I received when I asked him to fuck my ass. "Please," I begged. "I want to know what that's like."

The hypocritical thing is that it's not as if the thought itself troubles him. I know he's done it before. Early on, he told me when we were at that share-everything point in our relationship. You show me yours and I'll show you mine. So I know full well that he ass-fucked some gorgeous girl in New York. Long time ago, sure, but he's done it. Yet he won't do it with me. There are things you just don't do with the girl you're going to marry. According to him, that is. According to his beliefs, there are ways you don't play with the mother of your future children. So he won't do those things with me.

You will.

You don't have any preconceived notions of who I'm supposed to be. Or why I shouldn't behave in a particular way. If I were to come to your house tonight, sneak away for longer than expected, you'd make me tremble simply by eyeing my body. By gazing at me with your jaw set, as if you were trying to decide which part to devour first. Which part to tie up, or spank, or fuck. Which part to bend over, or kiss, or shoot your come on. But you'd choose after a moment's contemplation, and whatever you chose would make us both climax. Because you know me. You know me so fucking well that I don't even have to think when we're together. I just put myself in your hands and let you guide us.

So I'm well aware of the fact that when we were finished, for the first time of the evening, at least, you'd take me to the shower and scrub the sin away, and then you'd press me up against the cool black tiles and fuck it right back in me.

Because deep down inside, we both know what *he* doesn't know, what he'll never know: that I'm way too dirty to clean.

Machine Wash Hot

Sometimes I'm ashamed to admit it. Sometimes I feel really, really guilty. After all, I'm a socially responsible girl. I'm concerned about the environment. I use phosphate-free non-perfumed detergent, sure, but what about the water? What about the power? What about the noise pollution? For that matter, what about the steam rolling out of the garage, pulsing down the street and contributing to global warming? Do you have any idea what water vapor in the air is doing to our environment?

I'm embarrassed. Sometimes. Occasionally. Well, very occasionally. Not much of the time, really. Just every now and then, when I have a stab of self-doubt about my laundering practices.

It's my one serious extravagance, a shameless act of self-indulgence in a spacious household filled with tea-tree oil soap, all-natural window cleaner, fragrance-free dishwashing detergent and organic drain cleaner that doesn't work.

It's my one shameful, filthy little guilty secret:

Sometimes I run a load when nothing's really dirty.

Then again: I guess there's always something dirty at my house. Even if it's only my mind.

I make sure to load everything evenly, because there's nothing worse than having the washing machine do that ka-thump ka-thump ka-thump thing right in the middle of the spin cycle. Like they say on the inside of the lid, it could even cause injury.

Cottons are definitely my favorites—jeans, sweats, towels. They're heavy and hold water, and they give the machine that extra special uumph. The problem is that it's a fairly new machine, so it's pretty well insulated. That means the metal never gets really hot, and it never really does it for me to have it on warm. I love the feel of the warmth against me, and so I have to wash my cottons on hot. As a result, I don't really have many clothes left. My jeans are always too tight, and my cotton thongs tend to fray and disintegrate after just a couple of months.

But it's worth it, to feel the machine heating up underneath me, to feel the warm caress of the smooth white metal. The heat isn't what does it, though. It's a nice feature, but it ain't the heat, it's the motion. It's usually about five minutes into the cycle that it really starts to *spin*.

When I started, I'd use a pillow, draped over the corner. I'd wear tight jeans and a thong, and spread my legs around it. Now I don't even bother with the pillow. I just perch atop the machine. Usually, I do it sitting on top with my legs dangling over the side. Other times I get up close and personal, spreading around the corner. My favorite pants to wear when I'm doing that are my heavyweight, all-cotton sweats. But jeans work just fine, especially tight ones. Loading evenly is extra important if I'm going to go that route, though—in that position, a sudden, unexpected ka-thump could put me out of commission for weeks.

The spin cycle is six minutes long. That's always long enough for one, but sometimes not quite enough for two. Once I managed three, though. Washable wool.

I've gotten into the fetish of it; it turns me on to load the washer and then slowly strip my clothes off, leaving on just a bra and panties, then stuff the clothes in the cylinder and close the lid. I start the water and lean against the machine, waiting.

When I first began, I would fantasize, but I don't even need to do that any more. I get turned on just *smelling* laundry soap. Just walking into the garage excites me. The scent of clean clothes inspires a warm afterglow, and the clink of quarters arouses me just on general principle. Sometimes I walk past a laundromat and I have to go home and change my underwear. The one time the power was out at home, I did try to do my laundry in a laundromat. Now *that* was a disaster. I leaned against the washing machine as it fired into the spin cycle. I put my face against the metal as it vibrated, like a lover I couldn't touch. I sighed softly, languishing as the single mothers and college students looked at me like I was a maniac.

But at home, I climb on top and lean back against the machine, feeling the faint shiver as the cylinder fills with water. I feel it start to agitate, working back and forth in a rapturous kind of foreplay.

Then, when I feel the spin cycle start, I let out a little moan.

I lean back or hunker forward. I've gotten very limber; I can drape my knees over the side so I can press my pussy down hard against the machine. But that's not even necessary; the vibrations can travel through my tailbone and into me if I lean back, gently pinching my nipples as the rhythm mounts.

The machine pulses and shudders, fucking me with its cadenced motion. It goes faster, faster as the sensations build in me. And somewhere there, in the midst of the spin cycle, I come.

Until today. I'm spread, leaning forward, my pussy pressed against the warm metal, my body twisted. I feel like a gymnast on the parallel bars.

I'm close. Really close. I'm imagining the machine fucking me like some industrial-age behemoth, careless to anything but its own functions, fucking me as a side-effect of its purpose in life.

I'm on the edge. Right on the edge.

When the machine cuts out and spins down.

"Nnnnnnooooo!" I shriek, getting down off the machine and popping the lid. I move the clothes around and close the lid, its clank hollow in the steamy garage.

Nothing.

I move the clothes around some more. I shouldn't have loaded all those jeans. I take a pair of jeans out, throw them over my shoulder, close the lid.

Nothing.

"Come on, work with me, here," I say. I grab a wad of clothes—panties, bras, T-shirts—and toss them on the garage floor.

I pop the dial in, out, in, out, in, out, in, out.

Nothing.

"Nnnnnnooooo!" I want to cry. I really want to cry. I shift uncomfortably, my clit swollen and pulsing, my underwear matted and conformed to my pussy. I push my nipples against the cold metal, almost weeping.

I rush to the phone book, dial the number for AAAA Appliance Repair.

"We might be able to send someone out tomorrow," the perky operator tells me.

"No, you don't understand," I plead. "It's an emergency. You've got to send someone today."

"Is it a safety emergency? Is there a safety risk?"

"Oh, hell yes," I say. "Definitely."

"Like a fire risk? Can you smell smoke?"

I open my mouth to make up a story—flames shooting out of my beloved washer, smoke everywhere. "No," I sigh miserably.

"I'm afraid we're all scheduled up. Perhaps you could go to a laundromat?"

"No, I can't—I don't have time—I mean, I'm leaving for,

um, Europe tonight. I'm going out of the country. I don't have time to go to a laundromat."

"I'm sorry, Ma'am, there's nothing I can do. I can send someone tomorrow."

"That will be fine," I sigh, my voice breaking with tears.

"I thought you said you wouldn't be there tomorrow."

"Someone will be home," I say miserably. "Just...please, as soon as possible."

"Tomorrow at 3:00?"

"Fine." I hang up and hurl the phone across the room.

Throwing myself across the bed, I reach underneath and pull out the white plastic wand. I look at it with distaste. It's covered with a thin film of dust. I strip off my underwear, wipe the head of the wand off with my panties. I spread my legs, picturing the washing machine, and press the vibrator to my clit.

Five minutes later, I'm staring at the ceiling, frowning.

I read an article once on "vibrator addiction." I guess this is like that. When I went to the sex shop, they told me this was the strongest vibrator made. Whoop-de-friggin' do. I shut my eyes tight, try to picture the hottest guy I can imagine. He's got dark hair, pale blue eyes, full lips, no clothes at all and an enormous cock, but what I'm more interested in is his tongue—Gene Simmons meets Angelina Jolie. In my fantasy, he stands there, a blank look on his face, unsure what to do.

It's been so long I don't really remember what goes where. I remember the tongue; that feels good. I'm pretty sure I could still come that way, but when I press the vibrator hard to my clit and imagine this fantasy man going down on me, blah blah blah. I stare blankly at the ceiling.

Then I imagine him crawling on top of me, entering me.

For some reason, that does it. I start to get turned on. I wriggle on the bed, wishing the sensations were stronger but getting turned on by the thought of my fantasy man inside me. I shut my eyes tight. I'm excited, but the sensations of the vibrator on my clit are just kind of annoying me.

I switch the vibrator off and sigh.

I guess I didn't hear the buzzer at first, over the buzz of the vibrator. There's someone at the door, leaning hard on the buzzer. God, I hate it when people do that. If I don't answer after one buzz, why the hell do they think I'm going to bother to answer after ten?

I jump up and reach for my robe, the little silk one I wear around the house. I should wear the terrycloth one to answer the door, I know, but I'm much too annoyed to bother looking for it. Oh, that's right. It's in the washer.

I can't find the belt of my little silk robe. I hold it closed and go to the door.

You're already back in your truck, thinking I wouldn't answer. It takes me a moment to register what it says on the side of the van. Quadruple-A.

I run down the concrete path, reaching the side of the van just as you put it in gear. I knock desperately on your window.

When you turn your eyes toward me, I melt. They're pale blue, flashing brightly in contrast to your dark hair. Your full lips are twisted downward, confused. Why is this woman in a sexy little robe pounding on your window? You lean over, crank the window down.

God, those lips are incredible. You fix me with a confused stare. Then you smile, and I smile back, wanting those lips.

"I'm sorry," I say. "I was about to get in the shower. Are you the repairman?"

"They said it was an emergency. You're on your way out of the country?"

Maybe it's the intense way you look at me, the vague interest I register in your gaze as it flickers over my face, my shoulders. I realize my hair is messed up, I haven't showered, I'm sweaty. I realize the neighbors can see me in my tiny little robe, the way it barely reaches below my ass. I feel ashamed, embarrassed, but somehow turned on, knowing you've taken even that quick look of interest. God, you're gorgeous. I was so turned on when you rang the bell, maybe I'm just not my usual self. But I want to feel those full lips against me.

"Yes," I say. "I'm leaving the country. I need to do my laundry."

"Evidently," you say with a smirk. "I worked an early shift, so I'm just finishing up now. I told them I could come by and take a look at your appliance."

"Yes," I say. "I'd really appreciate that."

When you get out of the car, I can't decide if I'm gratified or offended to see your eyes taking in my whole body. I clutch the robe more tightly closed. You're tall, muscled, your shop shirt unbuttoned just far enough to show me your white undershirt and the hair on your chest. I lead you into the house and to the garage, wondering if you're still looking at me, if you're noticing how short the robe is in back.

You step over the sodden jeans and panties in the middle of the floor. Is it my imagination, or does your gaze linger just a bit on the twisted shape of the most lacy underthings sprawled on the concrete? I feel myself begin to redden slightly.

"What's the problem?"

"It just....stopped. Right in the middle of the spin cycle." I have to fight not to bury my face in my hands and sob, tell you the whole story. That, I feel, would be wholly inappropriate.

I stand there awkwardly, watching you work. When you bend forward, I see you've avoided plumber's butt by wearing a pair of clean white boxer shorts. Calvin Klein's.

For some reason that's sexy to me. Rather than going inside to put some clothes on, I stand watching you work. There's something sexy about how you start to diagnose my machine, how you lean over and wrench it away from the wall like it was no effort at all to move that enormous device loaded with water and wet panties. I feel my breath catch as I watch your muscles bunch under the tight shop shirt.

"Wow, it's hot in here," you say. "Mind if I take this off?"

I want to laugh; it could have come from a bad porn movie. But I do *not* mind if you take it off, not at all. I've been wondering what you look like with just that undershirt on.

"No," I smile. "Go ahead."

You slip off your cotton-poly shop shirt, toss it across the dryer. I look at the discarded gray garment, moist with your sweat. Machine wash warm with like colors. Tumble dry low. Then, when I can't resist it any longer, I look at your shoulders. God, they're wide. You must work out. Or maybe it's just moving around giant machinery stuffed with women's underthings that makes you so buffed.

You glance over at me, seeming annoyed that I'm watching you work.

"So where are you going?"

I think you're telling me politely to leave. As in, "Are you going to the bedroom, the kitchen, the back yard, lady? Anywhere but fucking *here*." I stare at you blankly.

"Your trip. You said you were leaving the country."

"Oh, that!" I giggle nervously, feeling my face redden further. "Oh, it's...it's nothing, really....nothing at all."

"Where to?"

"Oh, you know," I say, toying nervously with my hair. "Spain...and...you know, Spain...and....and Portugal....maybe, oh, I don't know, northern Italy or maybe France or something...."

"Where in Spain?"

I search my mind for a city, but none is forthcoming. "You know, wherever the mood takes me. I'm very much a free spirit." Then it hits me, and I cry out like an idiot. "Madrid!" Then, "Barcelona! Seville! The, um, the Basque region." Weakly, I mumble, "You know....wherever."

"Wow, one of those Eurail vacations. Those are great. I spent a lot of time riding the rails myself."

"Riding the rails?" I shift uncomfortably.

"On trains," you say. "You know, in Europe."

"Oh, you've been to Europe?"

You laugh, give me something that would be a sour look if you didn't seem amused. "Believe it or not. A washing machine repairman." You've got the front panel opened now, and it excites me to see the guts of my machine. "I was an exchange student for a year. In college."

"College?"

"Yeah. World Literature and Cultural Studies. Did you go to school?"

The small talk continues as you explore the machine's inner workings. I keep pulling the tiny robe closed, pressing my thighs together tighter, acutely aware that I'm stark naked underneath. But I don't want to break the spell you've cast by going inside to get dressed. I keep chatting with you, noticing after fifteen minutes that my nipples are still quite hard, and that you can see them clearly through the robe. When I cross my legs I feel the lips of my pussy sliding smoothly together, moist.

"See, there's your problem right there," you say. "The lubricant well has run dry. See, it happens when you get out of balance—everyone does it, mind you, it's built into the system, but it does cause your lube to leak out sometimes, kind of run down inside. Causes excess friction, especially when you're right in the middle of a serious spin, and you just burned right up—did you smell smoke?"

"What? Oh...yes, definitely. Smoke." I shift from foot to foot nervously.

"Yeah, see, that'll cause smoke. Not fire, mind you, just a slow, nasty smolder. Bad for the belts, you see. Gets real hot in the center here, and next thing you know, everything's gone to shit. Pardon my french. Do you wear cottons?"

"Excuse me?" My eyes are wide, fixed on you, on the way your undershirt clings to your muscled body. "Did you say 'cottons'?"

"Cottons. Do you wash a lot of cottons?"

"Uh...you know, cottons, silks...lace.... I mean....satin...um, would you like something to drink?"

"Thanks, maybe later. I'm going to have to take your machine with me."

"Oh....really...." I want to feel my heart breaking, but I'm more interested, all of a sudden, in what you will look like wrestling it into the back of your van. I smile weakly, suppressing the urge to say "Can I watch?"

"Can I open your door?"

"Excuse me?"

"Your garage door. Does it open?"

"Oh. There's an opener. The button's by the side door."

You smile at me, and I can't tell if it's knowing or clueless. But I see your eyes flicker down over my legs again, then linger for a split second on the place where I've pulled my white silk robe into a V between my breasts. My nipples are still visible through the thin silk.

"Thanks," you say. Your full lips look beautifully kissable.

You get a dolly from the truck. I run back to my bedroom, planning to hide until you're gone. But I can't resist the temptation of watching you wrestle my beloved machine onto your dolly. At the last minute, I kick the vibrator under my bed, along with my dirty, frayed thongs scattered across the floor.

You've got your arms around it, your muscles straining as you walk it back and forth. The machine makes satisfying, echoey *thumps*.

"You'll have to wring them out," you say, nodding toward the basket. "I'm afraid they're really wet."

"Oh," I say. "That's fine...." I'm entranced by the way your shoulders look, bunching with the exertion. I catch my breath when you let out a manly groan, walking the machine onto your dolly. You bend over to slide the strap under; I see your boxers again and wonder what you look like in them, without the jeans. And maybe without the boxers.

You cinch the strap down and pull it tight into the cradle.

"I've got some things for you to sign," you say. "We should make an appointment for when you get back."

I stiffen. "An appointment?"

"For me to return your machine. It'll only take a week to fix. You'll be gone."

"Excuse me?"

"In Spain."

"Oh, that. Yes, I'll be gone. In Spain."

"When do you get back?"

"Oh, you know....whenever...."

"A free spirit, like you said." You smile. "I like that."

I watch you as you tip the machine back onto your dolly and walk it around my driveway. I know you're probably wondering why I came out of the garage and stand there watching you load it, nervously clutching my robe closed. Or maybe you're *not* wondering.

You come back with a clipboard. "Your John Hancock right here, please." You call me by name—no "Miss," no "Ms.," no "Ma'am." Just my first name, and I love the way your full lips form around it.

You're sheened with sweat, your undershirt soaked. You're breathing a little hard. Me, too.

"Would you like something to drink?" I ask you.

"Well, I'm off duty as soon as you sign those papers," you smile. "A cold drink would be great."

"I've got some beer in the fridge."

"That would be perfect."

I have no idea how old the beer in the fridge is—I don't usually drink the stuff, and it's left over from a party. I get two of them and come back into the dining room to find you seated at the table.

"I really appreciate it," you say, taking a pull at the beer. "It's been a long day."

"I imagine."

"You live here all alone?"

"Yes," I say. "All alone." I have to resist the urge to blurt out "with my washing machine." Instead, I say nervously: "So tell me about Spain."

As you speak, I watch your lips, focusing on the way your tongue lazes out to lick them as you speak. You're still wearing your undershirt, soaked with sweat. I can smell you, sharp in my living room, the scent of your exertion on my behalf. I breath deep. I take a pull on the beer. It's cheap and stale, six months old, but you're not complaining. You're telling me about Spain, about your time travelling around on Eurail. You're telling me how beautiful Spanish women are, and how you hope that doesn't sound disrespectful.

"No," I say breathlessly. "It doesn't sound disrespectful at all."

"Are you Spanish?"

I blush, looking down. I feel myself smiling, almost against my will. I hear a girlish giggle, not believing that it could have come from me.

Are you a cad? A lascivious mechanic going from house to house preying upon weak-willed women who have lost their favorite path to sexual satisfaction? Or an angel of mercy, servicing lonely housewives in faceless suburban houses where the washing machines fuck them better than their husbands?

Or have you just been paying attention, watching the signs, picking up every clue I've dropped that I desperately want you, that if you leave before I've had you I'll be miserable, left with neither my favorite sex toy or the only man who can render it functional again. Have you noticed how I've been looking at you? That I didn't bother to put my clothes on? That I slipped into the bedroom to clean up a little before inviting you in for a beer?

I don't give a damn, really. You could be the Maytag Casanova for all I care. I could be one of a hundred women you've seduced with your talk of lubricants, spin cycles, washable cottons and overheating cylinders. The only thing I care about is that you've leaned closer to me, so close I can smell you strong enough to make my head spin faster than the cylinder when it's packed with hoochie-mama jeans.

"Because you're really very beautiful," you tell me.

I blush deeper. "I bet you say that to every girl with a broken washing machine."

"Only when I'm on overtime," you say, and your mouth comes for mine.

I let the silk robe fall open, not even caring that there's nothing on underneath. Your lips feel full against mine, the taste of your tongue rich and inviting. I feel your hands on my breasts, fingertips grazing them. I put my arms around you and your body feels hot, exciting. I fall into your arms.

Your arms go around me and I feel your hands on my buttocks. Your hands come slowly up my back and you pull the robe off of me. It falls discarded on the kitchen table. I snuggle into you as you kiss me some more, and I can feel the bulge in your pants growing as I rub my naked body against you.

I take your hand and lead you toward the bedroom.

Is it just because you're fixing my washing machine? It's tempting to say so, but you're the most gorgeous thing I've ever seen. I lay on the bed nude and watch you while you take your clothes off. The undershirt comes over your head and I see your beautiful chest with its trace of dark hair. You kick off your shoes and step out of your pants, and I see those boxers that tempted me before. When you take them down I look at your cock, standing big and hard, and I'm hungry for it. When you come for me on the bed I get up onto my knees and reach for you, taking hold of your erect cock.

It slides easily into my mouth, tasting salty and sending a wave of desire through me. I bend over on my hands and knees, holding your shaft with my hand and running my tongue all over your head. You're beginning to leak pre-come and I lick it off, lifting my eyes to look into yours as you watch me sucking your cock. I reach my arms around you to pull you closer to me, my hands on your buttocks, and open wide, taking you all the way down.

You moan softly, your hips gently working back and forth as I slide onto you. I'm so turned on I can hardly stand it; I've got to have you inside me. I lavish my tongue all over your cock and rub it against my cheeks. Then I pull away, move back onto the bed, and lay, stretched, legs spread and arms over my head in an expression of helpless invitation.

I want you to fuck me.

You don't, though. You're not letting me off that easily. Instead, you climb onto the bed with your face at my crotch. I gasp as I feel your rough face between my thighs, five-o-clock shadow feeling dangerous and thrilling against my skin. Your tongue, though, is soft and tender, warm, then hard as it finds my clit and begins to lick.

My back arches, I claw at the sheets, and I hear myself moaning, loud. Your tongue works magic on me—god, how did you learn to eat pussy this well?

Your fingers discover the entrance to my pussy and slide inside, two of them, I think, slowly fucking me as your tongue keeps working. Your other hand comes up and touches my breasts, caressing them and pinching the nipples gently as I mount closer to orgasm. I'm going to come—I know I'm going to come.

You seem to sense that very moment of no return, when I'm on the edge of climax. You move faster than I expect. Your body comes up against mine, your cock sliding between my legs, your weight bearing me down as you enter me. That's all it takes, with the strength of your tongue having coaxed me so close; with the first touch of your cock, I come, moaning, twisting and writhing under your thrusting body. I rise to meet you as you push deep inside me, and I can feel the head of your cock reaching its deepest point inside me, your balls soft against my thighs as you fill me.

"Yes....yes..." I moan as you start to fuck me.

You've got incredible back muscles—must be from lifting all those washing machines. I don't care where the come from, I just care that your body is propelling your cock hard into my cunt, rhythmically, fucking me more perfectly than I've ever been fucked. I wrap my thighs around you, my legs trapping yours so I can feel every inch of your taut muscles as you strain to fuck me faster. You kiss my neck, your tongue tracing a path from jaw to ear, and whisper "I'm going to come." And that's when I do it, a second time, so rare, but so easy as I feel your cock sliding into me, its curve fitting me like a hand in a glove. My arms and legs pull you close and hard against me, and when you let out your groan I feel the tension of your body, feel my pussy accepting your come, feel you relax on the cushion of my body as you let yourself go inside me. Holding me, you kiss my neck, your teeth gently grazing the flesh.

It's almost dark, well after the end of your work shift. We lay there silently as the sky darkens outside my window.

Eventually, you kiss me again.

"Listen," you say. "I know you need to get some laundry done before your trip."

"What?"

"Your trip. You could do laundry at my place. I've got a washer/dryer."

I look at you blankly, and then I remember.

"When is it you're leaving for Spain, again?" you ask me.

I sigh. It wouldn't be right. Not now that you've let me know you, let me know the feel of you inside me, of your tongue on my clit, making me come. I can't just keep lying to you, can I?

"Let me tell you something about me and Spain..." I begin.

No Resistance

It's the bricks that get to me. The hard, chipped dirt-red wall of bricks. My hands are flat against that wall, and from this close-up vantage point I can see every crack, every crevasse. You're more interested in an entirely different crevasse, the slippery wet one between my thighs. Now, you're UP against me, pushing me into the wall with each thrust. First one hard, firm thrust, and I catch my breath, dragging in the night air, filling my lungs with the city smell of the alley behind the dance club.

I couldn't get in tonight. Too young to drink, too young party with the rest of the jubilant crowd inside, but that doesn't matter, because I'm definitely old enough to fuck. You carded me at the door, that insolent look in my green eyes winning me exactly nothing from you. No admission. No way. You glanced at the fake ID that said I was twenty-three years-old, as of last week. And yeah I'll be twenty-three, sure. In three more years. You looked me up and down, and smiled slightly, smiled with your eyes even as you were shaking your head, No. Sorry, baby. But you weren't saying no to everything, were you? Just to letting me in the bar.

After that, my friends didn't even bother to try their luck. Their IDs were even less believable than mine, and they headed back to the car, off to an apartment where an impromptu party was already in progress.

"Come on," they called to me, but I didn't want to go.

"I'll get a cab," I said, and they shook their heads. Why would I want to hang around downtown, when I couldn't get into anywhere but Double Rainbow? Was I really so pure that an ice cream cone would take the place of a vodka tonic?

I had my reasons. Because when you handed me back my ID, you leaned in close and said, "I'm off in ten."

Those were magic words. Because here's the truth: I didn't want to go to the club, anyway. That was all my friends' idea. I'm not into the drinking scene. Not big on dancing crushed together with a mob of people I don't know. I wanted something else. Plain and simple, I wanted you. But how was I supposed to get your attention without standing in line? I've seen you out here, on your stool, playing guard to the bar. And I've watched you, the way you look at people, sizing them up. You know exactly what you're doing, which I respect, but you also look as if you know how do a whole range of other, more interesting things. If you can nail someone like me so quickly, what else could you know about me, just from looking into my eyes?

Simple. One look. One guess, and you had my wrist captured firmly in your hand and led me around to the back of the bar, pushed me forward, so that you could admire me from behind. You took your time, making me feel as if I were really on display. You clucked your tongue against the roof of your mouth as you gazed at the curves of my ass and hips under the sheer, summer-weight dress that I'd agonized about. Tonight, I chose silver—T-shirt style, over black fishnet stockings that stay up without a garter belt. You slid the dress up, high, revealing my secret weapon—no panties. And then you said, "Oh, man," and I looked over my shoulder at you, seeing the first sign of your ability to be moved.

No panties is what got to you. It's what made you harder than hard. Harder than steel. It's what made you bend down on your knees on the asphalt and press your face to the split of my body from behind. Licking me there. Drawing forth the slippery sex juices with the heady wet heat of your mouth. That's what got to you.

But it's the bricks that get to me. The hardness in front of my face while your hardness slides between my thighs. The 'no resistance' of the bricks. I can push as hard as I want to with the palms of my hands, and I will get exactly nowhere. The wall is set. My body is the only thing here that's going to give. Sweetly. Easily. Your cock slips back and forth, driving hard inside me. I groan, lowering my head for a moment to stare down at my deep red-painted toenails in the open-toed sandals. I need to steel myself, need to catch my balance, but I can't.

Everything feels too good this evening. Too right.

The way you push in, and then pull back out again, leaving me empty and craving. The way you reach one hand in front of my body to stroke my clit, to strum your fingers against it in the exact rhythm as the beat emanating from the bar band. We can hear it all. The music, the laughter, the partying. But we're not a part of it. We are on our own, an island of two, and that's fine. Two is all we need.

The feel of your jeans against my thighs makes me moan again. The fact that we're both mostly dressed while we do this. I love how hard you want to fuck, and yet how slow you're taking this. Even though we're out in public. Even though we could be caught, spotted, at any moment. You don't rush. You just glide in and out, teasing me all the while with your knowledgeable fingers. And then you move in even closer, so that you can use both hands between my legs. Parting my pussy lips wide, as you slide in deep again. I can't believe how sexy it feels to be opened like that. The night air on me. The rush of it on that wettest of skin. Then your thumb tricks over my split again, and I know I'm moments from coming. Sheer sweet moments.

And when you grip my waist and pull me hard down on you, I hear you sigh again, because you realize exactly what you've come up against: no resistance.

Runner's High

You've wondered aloud about it, about why we always have our very best sex in the mornings, especially after I exercise. When you ask me, I blush and turn away. I usually make some self-consciously raunchy comment about morning wood, about how boys like sex in the morning, don't they? So why shouldn't girls? Or I mumble an excuse and change the subject, maybe making a silent resolution to come on to you in the evening to throw you off the scent of my secret.

Now I've decided to tell you the truth, but you have to promise not to tell, because it's naughty. It's a little silly, maybe even. I guess it's kind of embarrassing.

But it really, really makes me wet.

Every morning when I go for my run, I imagine it's you making me do it. You are my merciless master, and you love making me exert myself. Sure, partly this is because I'm a lazy exerciser and I'd always find a good excuse not to run. Turning a workout into a sex game makes it more interesting. But there's more to it than that. I do it because it excites me to think of you making me sweat, strain, exhaust myself.

I slide nude out of the bed where you're still sleeping comfortably. I give a longing look to your cock, often hard as you sleep, the mystery of morning wood. I always want to reach out and take it in my hand, slide my mouth down over it—but it's far more exciting to wait. I know that hard-on will be waiting for me when I return, when I'm slick with the sweat of my ordeal and my blood is pumping, my body aching for sex.

I put my long hair in a ponytail, step into my skintight bicycling shorts, and pull on my sports halter always matching the colors—white shorts with white halter, black shorts with black halter—because looking good is part of the game. I pull a tight spandex jersey over my head, knowing it will be cold out there until I work up my own heat. The faint sound of your breathing from the bed is a whispered order from your throne.

Feel the burn, you order me. *Keep going until you can't take any more—and then go harder*. You're merciless. You're evil. You're dirty.

I take out my Walkman and put in a tape, the same rhythmic industrial band we play when we're making love. I fix the Velcro strap around my hand, put the earphones in my ears. I close the door behind me, start the tape, and run.

The morning air is sharp with cold. I shiver as I think of you watching me.

The first mile is always the hardest. As the beat pounds through me, the dull thud of my feet matching it perfectly, I can feel your hand on my ass, spanking me as you run alongside me, never letting me slow down. The pain builds as I feel the sweat break out on my face and body. Sweat dribbles down into the small of my back, soaks the sports bra and jersey till they wick it away and my scent releases on the breeze. I feel my heat building further, to the point where I'm uncomfortable. Every ounce of pain is like a torture you've devised for me. I pass men and women on the sidewalks and people driving their VWs and Audis to work. My public suffering is a specific torment you've designed for me: Everyone can see my submission to you. Everyone in the world knows I belong to you.

I'm starting to overheat when you mercifully force me to strip. Feeling unseen eyes on me, I pull the zippered spandex jersey over my head and tie it around my waist. The morning cold hits me hard, and I feel my nipples stiffening in the white sports bra, evident to anyone who cares to look, for you've decreed that I'll have no privacy, that my naked body is to be enjoyed by all. This only makes my nipples harder, harder than the cold could ever make them, and as they grow more erect I feel more and more exposed. I can sense my pussy throbbing, its staccato rhythm much quicker than the pulse of the industrial music filling my ears, much harder than the drum-machine explosions. I know from experience that my spandex shorts, hugging the lips of my bare pussy, are growing wet with much more than sweat, as the scent of my desire for you soaks the material. Wicked away on the wind, the scent travels to anyone on the street who cares to draw a breath, and at your decree I am further exposed to them—now they know just how wet I am, just how much it turns me on to suffer for my master. My face is flushed with more than physical exertion, and the tops of my breasts feel hot despite the morning chill.

I am in agony. Every step is torment, you egging me on as I press myself forward. I imagine you driving alongside me in the car, cracking your whip every time I slow, every time I contemplate stopping. I desperately wish I could let go of this torture and sit down at a bus stop to rest. But you won't let me; your whip strikes its mark each time, ripping the sports bra into shreds. Perhaps it falls off, and I run bare-breasted through the streets as I hear the gunshot cracks of your whip. I push myself to run faster. I force myself to stop wishing I could rest. I savor the burning feeling in my muscles and pick up speed.

As I reach deep down inside myself to find the stamina that will please you, you order me to stop; your next order, in my fantasy, is to remove my spandex shorts. Obeying reluctantly, I leave them and let the shorts and my spandex jersey join the tatters of my sports bra in the gutter. At your command, I resume my run, traveling sweat-slick, flushed and naked through the streets—naked except for my tape player, which pulses with the rhythm of you fucking me.

Men and women look over my sweaty, naked body, see me flushed with exertion. I feel my pussy throbbing harder, wetter as my juices run down my thighs—and then I'm through the pain, the suffering over, the pleasure just beginning. You drive alongside me as I head back to our house.

I let myself back in the silent cottage, smelling the musk of your sleeping body. I can never wait. I always strip off my damp sports bra in the living room, kick off my shoes and socks in the kitchen as I get a glass of water, peel off my soaked shorts in the hall as I head toward the bedroom.

You've sprawled across the bed to take over my side as well as your own. You're naked under the sheet, the damp white material clinging to the curves of your body. Naked now myself, as naked as I was when I ran through the streets for your pleasure, I slip under the sheet, feeling the heat engulf me, and I start kissing your neck. You awaken after the first few kisses, and for an instant I think you're going to stop me. But you don't. I lick my way down to your hard cock and take it into my mouth, suckling as you gasp and moan slightly.

I caress your balls gently with my hand and continue working your cock in and out of my mouth as my pussy hums in anticipation. You're close, your morning hard-on bringing you near to orgasm right away. I can sense it in the way your muscles tense, and I let your cock slip out of my mouth, already slick. I cradle its hardness in my hand as I gently ease your legs apart, and slide down to the end of the futon until my waist is bent, my knees just reaching the floor so I can kneel to lick your balls. You moan softly as I stroke your cock with my hand and feel your delicate balls against my tongue; I know I could bring you off in an instant, but now *I'm* in charge, and I'm going to make you wait. When you've cooled down a bit, I lick back up to your cock and descend on it hungrily, my mouth easily opening up for you, my lips coming almost all the way down your shaft. You groan. I pump you into my mouth and moan softly myself, low in my throat, loving the taste of your cock.

Smoothly, my body feeling chilled with the sweat evaporating from it, I twist my body atop yours and plant my knees on either side of your face. You discard the pillow on the floor as I spread wide and lower my pussy onto your mouth. Your mouth molds to my pussy as if you're famished, and I feel your tongue working into my folds as I fall on your cock with newfound eagerness, taking as much of it as I can. My hips work quickly with the motions of your tongue, and I'm very close to coming. You're close, too, but I'm still in charge. I take your cock out of my mouth and breathe warmly over it as you focus on my clit, devouring me.

I'm going to come, and you know it. You don't let up, wanting me to come on your tongue. I hold onto your cock as if it were my last hold on reality and I let out a moan as I feel my orgasm coursing through me, the pleasure overtaking my nude, sweaty body. Before I know it I'm pumping my mouth down on your cock again, hungry for your come as my climax heightens. But I stop myself just in time—I'm desperate to get fucked and I'm still in charge.

I switch positions on top of you, pressing my mouth to yours so I can taste the salty tang of my pussy. I press the head of your cock to my entrance and moan softly as it goes in. I'm so wet your cock slides right through me, my lips curving around the base as your shaft fills me. I start to pump you hungrily, anxious to feel your come inside me. It's only a few thrusts before you arch your back, coming, gripping my naked body hard to yours and shivering as you climax. I can feel its heat inside me, feel your thrusts intensify as I hold still atop you and let you fuck me until you're spent.

So now you know my secret. You know why the sex we have in the morning is so incredible, especially when I'm slick with sweat and exhausted. Of course, we would have incredible sex anyway, but this certainly doesn't hurt. And the next time you make a joke about how a civilized girl would never get out of bed that early in the morning, you'll know you're right. After all, is any of this really civilized?

Paddle Brush

If you notice that I've "accidentally on purpose" left my paddle brush on the edge of your nightstand, you don't let on. Usually, the heavy-handled brush resides in the bathroom, along with the rest of my girly beauty routine products—make up, body glitter, feather-light puffs in an array of pastels. But tonight I've brought the heavy, black-lacquered brush into our room and left it poised in faux innocence by your side of the bed. It rests cozily between a carafe of water and the books you're currently reading: Baudelaire's "Flowers of Evil." Bataille's "Story of the Eye."

As I slowly button the top of my silky silver pajamas I steal cautious glances in your direction. Do you see? Don't you? From your casual countenance, I have no idea, which is exactly how you like it. There is nothing from your expression to let me know whether you're interested in playing the way I want to tonight—the way I need to play, I should say. Because I do. I need this. I've been crazy all day with this nagging inner craving. I want you to bend me over. To punish me the way you know how to do so well. Yet I know if I ask, if I whisper exactly what I want, then more likely than not, you'll make me wait.

My shoulders sag slightly as I slide into the shimmery pj bottoms. Then I climb onto my side of the bed, flick out the lamp, and rest my head on the fluffy down pillow.

"Goodnight, sweetheart," I murmur, my voice low and deeply sad.

"Why do you think they call it that?" you ask from where you stand, right next to your bedside table.

"What?" I ask, raising up on one arm to glance in your direction. My heart's already racing, but I mentally admonish myself to play it cool. No sense in giving away everything too early. Yet I've never been much of a Poker player. You can always read my thoughts easily.

"A paddle brush," you say, hefting the tool in one hand, and instantly my pussy tightens in response to those simple words. "I mean," you continue, eyes on the brush instead of me, "'paddle' seems to imply something specific, doesn't it? Something so different from simply brushing—"

"Like what?" I ask, but I know. Oh, god, do I know.

You don't immediately answer me. Instead, you sit down on the edge of the mattress, playing with the brush between your hands. From experience, I know to wait until you give me the signal. Acting overly excited never works out in my favor. The more heated up I am, the longer you always make me wait to give in, to bend over, to behave. Finally, you look over at me and smile. I'm awash in shivers, but I manage somehow to hold your gaze. "Come on, baby," you say. "Come on over here and let me brush your hair."

Somehow, I make it over to stand in front of you, but my legs can't stop trembling and I have to anchor my bottom lip between my teeth. Each breath I take is huge and shuddering. You are icily calm to my ragged heat wave. You are sunshine to my tropical storm. Slowly, you drag the bristles through my long auburn hair. I stand up straight and tall, holding myself as still as I can. Each stroke of the brush brings forth a fresh wash of wetness between my legs. I wonder if you can sense my arousal, if you can actually smell the scent of my sex. How long will you make me wait? I have no idea.

When I am nearly out of my mind with nervous excitement, you set the brush down and bring me even closer to you. I smell the spice of your cologne, feel the warmth of your embrace. I take another breath and start to relax.

Every move you make seems carefully planned: the way you bend me over your sturdy lap, the way you wait before sliding my pajama bottoms down my thighs. There's a moment when you admire me in that position, before slipping one hand under the waistband of my pjs and pulling them down. Then you touch my panty-clad ass ever so gently before lifting the brush again. Your touch is admiring as you cup each of my cheeks and squeeze just so. I know just how much you like my ass, and I squirm as your thumb traces the split between my cheeks. Even through the filmy barrier of my panties, I feel that intrusion, and I blush, although you can't see. The heat in my cheeks seems to radiate outward. My face is on fire.

There is no warning, no admonishing to be still, to behave. You let me have the first few heavy strokes in rapid succession, before I can process anything. Before I can tell you "Wait—" But we both know full well that I won't tell you 'wait,' because I want this too much. I need this too badly. My skin stings instantly, but I don't cry out. I'm nowhere near the point of crying yet.

"My sweet baby," you whisper, as you set the brush down again and now slide my panties down my legs. "You want it on the bare, don't you? That's what you really want."

Can't talk. Can't think. Luckily, I don't have to. You know me too well.

"Don't you, pretty one?" you say, pushing me, making me play right. I understand in the hazy mess of my thoughts that you won't continue unless I tell you exactly what you want to hear.

"Yes," I finally answer. "Oh, yes."

And then you take pity on me and give me the spanking that I crave, the true punishment I deserve. The pain dissolves into pleasure with each stroke. The sound reverberates in the room around me. I want to own the blows of the brush on my naked skin. I want to memorize every single sensation, to learn it hard so that I'll remember for next time. But I know I'll fail. Each spanking I get is new. Every time you place me over your lap, I feel like a spanking virgin. The fear rushes up and envelopes me. The sweetness of release comes fresh and unexpected.

Each time the hard-wooden back meets my ass, I suck in my breath, then let it out in a rush between my teeth. This is my ultimate fantasy, my purest of daydreams come true. Being spread out over your sturdy lap as you firmly mete out the type of discipline that I love best—it's what makes everything right in my world.

I know that my skin is taking on a deep cherry-blush. I know that my body moves against my will, feet kicking up, as if I'm fighting to get free. But I don't want to get free. All I want is your hand anchoring me in place, and that brush spanking my naked ass, bouncing against my skin, and your voice admonishing me and telling me to try harder to be a good girl.

"Don't you want to?" you ask, in that sly tone of voice. "Don't you want to be my good girl?"

Oh yes. Of course I do. I want it more than anything else. At least, once I'm through being your bad girl, that is. *Then* all I want to do is be your good girl. To get down on my knees by the bed and open my lips. To suck your cock forcefully down my throat, bathing it with the wetness that awaits you. I've been so naughty and you've been so deliciously fair. Now, it's time for me to reward you. I revel in the heat of my ass and the warmth of my cunt as I do my best to please you. Because I know that I'll fail no matter how hard I try, and that you'll have to lift me back up and push me over the edge of the bed. That you'll spank me again, even harder this time, before thrusting your cock between my legs and fucking me the way I need to be fucked.

Take me hard. Take me fast. Take me all the way there, until my vision blurs with the pleasure that awaits me.

"Paddle brush," you say softly, after you've come. Then you heft the weight of it once again, and I watch with cautious eyes from my position on the bed. "Why do you think they call it that? Do they know that every girl who buys one will want her man to paddle her?"

I don't know about every girl. I just know about me.

And I know as I watch you lift the brush in your firm, steady hand, that I will raise my hips up to meet each blow, and soon the wetness will once again begin its sweet route down my thighs.

Hollywood Magic

You drive the same type of insanely sexy vintage truck that my high school boyfriend did way back in the 80s. I'm no hot-rod chicklet—you won't find me in front of the car magazines at the newsstand—but you don't have to be a machine-head to appreciate this type of vehicle—one of those classic old Fords, with the seductive curves, the high bench-style seat, and the smell of worn leather. Jesus, I remember that smell. The summer before I left for college, my boyfriend and I spent hours in his truck, spread out on the front seat, his body on mine, and the butter-soft leather beneath my ass. I remember everything about that truck. At this point, almost more than I remember about the guy. Now, he's been long reduced to a hazy blur in my memory. A *good* blur—blond and handsome, rugged and young. But his truck remains bold and clear in my head, and whenever I see another truck like it, I find my heart racing all over again.

You must know what I mean, because I can tell the truck does the same thing for you. When you step out of the cab, you always run your hand gently along the door, as if you're petting the metal, caressing the body. If trucks could talk, yours would purr. Yet I've got the feeling that your identity isn't wrapped up with your vehicle. I can tell from the way that you move, that you know how to hold your own. Don't have to hide behind something else to make you cool. You like the truck for what it represents, but it doesn't define you.

Still, in Hollywood, everything's about what you wear, not who you are. What you drive, not what you think. So I appreciate that old truck of yours, and the way I seem to find myself parking next to it at all my favorite haunts: Whiskey-a-Go-Go, The Viper Room, Belly. People who don't live here think L.A. is some sort of huge metropolis, when really it all boils down to just one tight neighborhood, where people run into each other again and again—until there really aren't any strangers any more.

You're at the places I am, and you don't flinch when I stare at you across the room. Instead, you make your way up to me, and you squint your eyes slightly, as if trying to place where you've seen me before.

"Everywhere," I say in answer to your silent question.

You nod. "We seem to be on the same rotation."

"You like it here?" I'm talking about this particular place, not the city, and you know it.

"What's not to like?" you respond with a shrug, but the tone of your voice lets me know that you've been here, and you've done that, and maybe you'd like to go somewhere else and do something else with me.

"Are you done?" I ask, because this is a working-type party, where people are supposed to look as if they're having a good time, while really everyone has ulterior motives. The motives to meet and greet the people who make decisions in places like this. Except those people are all too plastered at this point to remember anything tomorrow. Or else they're gone already, off to someplace even hipper than this one. A strip-bar filled with airbrushed babes. Meeting other people. Making other decisions.

"Done," you nod, "with this place, anyway," and then you wait for another beat, staring into my eyes, and I find myself blushing and looking away. Where are we going to go? I don't know, and I don't really care, as long as we get there in your truck. For me, this journey will be the destination.

You take my hand and we walk out of the club together,

past the valet boys standing in a tight clinch in the parking lot, out to the street, where you've parked right at the corner. You open the door and give me a hand up, and then I wait in the darkness of the cab until you open the driver's side. And in those few moments, I breathe in the smell, that vintage truck smell, and it takes me back in time. Once again, my heart goes screaming in my chest, and I find myself desperately aware of the fact that my panties are already dripping.

Forget the drive, I think. *Forget it all. Just spread me out here, take me right here.*

But then in a wave of self-preservation, I remember exactly where "here" is—on the busy street of Santa Monica Boulevard, speared by the lights of every passing car, by the observant glances of any nosy pedestrian heading toward the clubs lined up in a row. And although exhibitionism has its time and place, this is neither. So I sigh and try to keep myself contained as you start the car and head down the gleaming black strip of asphalt.

I think I know where you're going. If I have you pegged correctly, then you'll be taking a left and heading us up toward the Hollywood Hills. To Griffith Observatory.

I smile when I see that yes, I've nailed your plans, and I stare out the window as you reach for my hand again. For a moment, I think you're going to be sweet and old-fashioned and squeeze my fingertips. Or else you might make a play for a little preview taste of what's to come and run your hand along my body. Instead, you surprise me and take my hand and set it high up on your thigh. I feel the warm, worn denim, and I run my fingers up and down, up and down, dying to inch them over, to feel your hardness beneath the button-fly.

There is no denying how much I want you. How, if we were in a movie, I'd take control of the wheel and turn us, tires screeching, down the next side street, sliding the truck into whatever space I could find and hiking up my dress to let you know what I wanted you to do. But we're in real life here, where crazy behavior like that is not always rewarded, so I take a deep breath and draw my fingers in lazy spirals high up on your thigh. I feel the hardness of your muscles beneath the soft worn denim, and I imagine what it will feel like when my naked skin finally meets yours. It's an image I've visualized often since I first caught sight of you. I've got the idea that this preview will pale in comparison to the feature presentation.

The truck handles the curves of the road with ease, as if the vehicle has transformed into a fast-paced sportster, as if it's not an old dinosaur chugging up the road. Soon enough we're there, in a spot held perfectly in time. And we can see the view, and the world around us, the inky dark sky and the golden lights twinkling. Rather than get out—why would we need to get out?—you reach for me, and now my fantasies unfold, merging and blending with reality.

The scent of the car wafts around me. Below it is the scent of the two of us—clean and fresh, perfumed and oiled, and below that our skin. Just skin. I lean up on you, push my arms on the seat behind you, and feel exactly how turned-on you are when your body meets mine. We are still clothed, and I like that. Like the taking-our-time moments before the real fucking starts.

I press myself to you, sealing myself to you, and it's as if our bodies are kissing, interlocking even through the barrier of our outerwear. We press together like that for a minute, taking our time. Then you slip your hand into my panties, reaching there between my lips to feel the wetness, and when you nod your head I know you want me to take my panties off. I squirm out of your embrace to do so, slipping those silky underthings down my lean thighs and watching as you split the button fly of your jeans.

I'm back on top of you in a heartbeat. My pussy opens up and takes your cock deep inside me, and then I'm doing the work, riding you. Owning you. Driving you the way that you drive your truck. I take charge, working up and down on my thighs, in total control. We both know that I'm in the driver's seat, and that's fine with you. I can tell from the look in your eyes that you're perfectly happy letting me set the pace. I like the fact that my mind has a double-vision of this action. Yesterday and today. And even though I've been there before, and I've done this before, with you it's all new. The way I feel when you bring your hands to my breasts and rub your thumbs along my nipples, still hidden away under my dress and bra. The way I sigh when you reach to pull me even closer so that you can kiss me while we fuck.

Your mouth is hot on mine, and you work slowly, nibbling at me, even while your cock is throbbing hard and fast within me. I like that. Like how in control you are, even as I'm on top. I sigh as you keep kissing me, now turning my head so that you can lick against my neck. You draw your hands through my hair, cradling me as you bring my lips against yours another time.

I squeeze your cock each time you kiss me. Maybe you understand that. Maybe you're so in tune with me already that you've figured out how to make me go slower or faster, rougher or more gently just by the way you kiss me. And then I get it. You're the one driving, maneuvering those dangerous curves. You know all about handling a fine ride—and that's what I've become. You turn me on and take me for the sweetest spin.

Up I buck on your cock, and then down I slide. You have your hands around my waist now, helping, urging me on. Your thumb flicks over my clit, finding just the perfect spot to touch. I shiver as you work me, and I come when you kiss me again.

The night is alive with the traffic melody of Hollywood. With the silver celluloid memories of screen stars and movie magic. But we're here together, alone together, taking a little piece of pleasure and making it our own.

The Key

You knock, as a courtesy, but come in before I can call out. Even after you open the door, you just stand in the doorway for a moment, looking at me.

"Come on," I urge, wanting you to enter the room and shut the door quickly behind you. Wanting to stave off any idle office gossip by the hens who work up and down the hall. With a half-grin, you walk to the desk and sit in the padded swivel-chair next to mine.

"What'cha working on?"

"Just editing."

"I brought you something."

Coffee, as always. This time it's a double-espresso. On Tuesday it was a latte with extra foam. You choose different flavors and styles every time you see me, and I am delighted by even this minor surprise. In a teasing way, you say that my life is too boring, that I play it too close to the lines in my Filofax, while you like to keep me off-guard.

"And something else, too," you say, doubly surprising me by pulling a small box out of your pocket, the secret pocket on the inside of your faded leather jacket. While I watch, you place the box on the edge of my desk and then tap it with your fingers, drumming out a steady beat.

"What is it?"

"You'll have to see for yourself, won't you?"

I smile and turn in my chair to study the fine bones of your face, the smooth brow and golden-brown eyes that change when you look at me. Gently, you put your hands on the sides of my chair and rotate the whole thing toward you, turning it on the wheels and pulling both me and the chair closer to you. Every movement is graceful, unconscious, feline. You do difficult things without thinking twice, while I have a hard time getting my jacket on without the shoulder pads bunching up on me.

You continue to slide the chair forward until our legs are touching. I smile, then stop—from your expression, I suddenly sense that you have something serious to tell me.

"Twice a week isn't enough anymore," you say quietly. "I think about you all the time." With a sigh, you move your hands to my legs, just above my knees, resting them there on my gray flannel slacks, setting your hands on me as a precursor, an appetizer, of what is to come. I sigh at your touch, knowing that you're right: this is no longer a fling. I miss you fiercely when we are apart, the warmth of you, scent of you.

"It's not my birthday," I say, half-teasing, attempting to lighten the mood. We're so close now that my breath stirs the wayward lock of hair that always falls over your forehead. "It's not Christmas. Or even Valentine's day."

"Just a present," you tell me, flashing me your unique smile, imperfect only because of one slightly chipped front tooth—that flaw makes me love you more "just because I wanted to."

Again, you tap the thin, flat box for emphasis, and then push it along my desk until it rests against my coffee cup. Then you take my right hand and turn it up so that you can kiss my palm, tracing your tongue along those delicate, near-dainty lines worn well into my palm, the map that tells a future I'm not sure I want to know. *Am I ready for it?*

"Should I open it now?" I ask, "or after?"

"After," you grin, dipping and swirling your tongue around each one of my clear-polished fingernails. "After."

*****

When you leave, I look at the present again. It's wrapped in red paper and tied with a tiny satin ribbon. I stroke the shiny paper and glossy black satin. Then I slip the box into the top drawer of my desk, turn off my computer, and get ready to go home. As I grab my trench coat from the rack, I imagine what might be inside the mystery gift. Until I open it, I can dream of the contents nestled safely within the box.

What if it held the key to freedom, I wonder. *Wouldn't that be nice? Wouldn't that be magic?*

"You're gonna watch me," you say, "Watch me eat your pussy, lick the cherry juices off your inner lips, slide my tongue inside your cunt...deep inside you there, where you're all warm and secret and safe. Baby, I want you to watch."

I take a deep breath, a ragged breath, listening to you on the other end of the phone line while rubbing myself on the edge of my chair. I wish I could talk back, but I'm suddenly shy, blushing like a teenager, even though I'm the older one in this relationship. I open my lips to speak, but the words won't come out of my mouth—I can't even formulate them in my mind.

"I'm gonna fuck you," you say, and I moan, thrilling at the urgency in your voice, the borderline desperation. "Gonna fuck my working girl, my good girl."

I sigh again, and realize, as the phone shakes in my hand, that I'm trembling.

"I'll bend you over your desk, lift up your skirt—you'll wear a skirt for me, won't you, darling? Not one of your power suits."

"Uh huh." There, that's something, "Yes, I will."

"I'll lift it up, exposing you, your legs, thighs, ass, your beautiful, creamy white ass."

And then? Then? Oh, please tell me, please talk to me. I want to record your voice in my head to play back at night, when I'm in bed next to him, when I'm awake and alive and on the verge of . . .

"I'm gonna fuck you, baby, hard and fast, just like you want it, just like you *need* it, fuck your sweet slippery pussy until you scream. I'll thrust into you and make you come over and over again. You are my bad girl, and I want to make sure that you understand that. And when I do, you'll be so loud for me, you will scream and moan and sob . . . and everyone's gonna know."

Everyone. Everyone's gonna know. What will they say? What can they possibly say?

"Did you hear the latest? She had a lover in her office, just last Tuesday. You must have seen him, younger, butch, rugged. You must have noticed him bringing coffee twice a week, as if he worked at Dante's Cafe. *As if.* He closes the door and stays in there with her, for much too long, much longer than it takes to get a buck seventy five out of your purse."

"Not her. I don't believe it. She's a good girl, a *good* girl. And she seems so, well . . . boring. Not too be cruel, or anything, but she is sort of mousy. You know?"

"That's only because of the way she dresses. She shouldn't wear so much gray, someone should take pity and tell her."

Pause and laughter. Two toilets flush.

"Well, maybe gray is sexy to some men. It sounds as if she's getting more than you are, Meredith."

"*You* should talk, Joyce. You're more of a slut than she is."

Giggling, then, "Bitch."

"Do you think her husband knows? Shouldn't someone tell him? To save the poor soul some pain."

"'Poor soul'? I don't think *that* man can feel pain. Didn't you see him at the Christmas party? The way he bossed her around. He's a bad dream, a nightmare. A neanderthal."

More wild laughter partially drowned out by the splashing of running water.

Then: "That's a great color lipstick on you."

"Thanks, it's new. Russet Moon. Chanel."

The bathroom door whooshes open and then closed, and I put my feet back down on the blue tile floor and smile to myself—though, honestly, shouldn't I be crying?

You knock, as a courtesy, but come in before I can call out. Still, what would I say? *"Enter, baby,"* the way you talk. *"Come and fuck me against the wall. Tear off my clothes, my good work shoes, my Jones New York blazer, my hundred and eighty nine dollar Ann Taylor dress. Fuck me like a locomotive, let me feel . . . anything, let me feel anything again. I'm so tired of being boring, gray, mousy, dead. I want to live again, in your kiss, in your embrace, in your fire."*

"My lovely lady, you look delicious." You seem to drink me in with your eyes, lifting up your black wayfarer sunglasses to get a better look. You brush the mahogany curls away from my forehead and kiss me there first, chastely, sweetly, and then you undo the top button of my red silk shirt and press two fingers in the indent there, to feel my pulse.

"This color suits you, darling. It makes you look like a fire cracker."

"Really? You think so?"

"Mm hmm." You undo the rest of my buttons, "It looks wonderful on you, but, truly, I think it will look much better on the floor."

I laugh—can't help it—and you unfasten the clasp of my black lace bra.

"And this," you say, helping me slip it off, "This is incredibly sexy."

"I know. Much better than the old-maid things I usually wear."

You get down on your knees in front of me, and slowly begin stroking my body, along my shoulders, across my naked breasts, and down my belly.

"Did you buy it for me?"

"No, not really."

You pause and look up at my face, misunderstanding, thinking that I'm seeing someone else. As if I could. Your eyes cloud with worry, with jealousy, but when I smile, reassuring you—"I bought it for myself"—you immediately continue where you left off, kneeling on the floor between my legs and cupping my breasts tenderly.

"I don't know why I wore those others for so long. I've always wanted to dress like this."

"You were scared of what you might unleash," you murmur against my warm flesh. "You were afraid you'd like it."

Then there's silence again as you kiss the valley between my breasts and down the flat curve of my stomach to the waistband of my skirt. Silence that hangs in the air around us—beautiful like a tapestry, it's filled with thoughts and dreams and fantasies, all of which are about to come true.

"You wore this for *me*, though, didn't you?"

"Yes," I sigh, and you motion for me to stand and then bend me over my desk, slowly lifting up the back panel of my floral skirt and exposing me from behind. You stroke me through my sheer nylons and then carefully peel them down my legs, helping me step first out of my shoes and then out of the stockings.

"You are exquisite," you whisper, "Such a vision. I can't wait to be taste you—"

They were wrong, those catty women in the bathroom. You have long been my admirer, my sweetheart, my obscene caller. You have kissed me and touched me, and we have indulged in "petting" like two high school kids, but never, not until this moment, have we actually made love.

You slip one hand under the elastic of my naughty lace panties, black ones to match the bra, and then pull them down to my ankles and leave them there, capturing me. I feel your hot breath on the inside of my thighs before your tongue begins the journey upward, parting my nether lips and diving inside me where I am so ready for your, so willing. My thighs are damp with my honey, and you flick and lick your tongue in circles, catching each drop, making sweet hungry noises as you devour me.

I grip the edge of my desk with both hands, digging my nails into the carved wood border. I bite my bottom lip to keep from crying out, and I wonder, belatedly, if you locked the door. But does it matter?

"Gonna make you scream," you say, soft and low, without moving your mouth from me. Your voice resonates within my pussy, vibrating amazingly inside me. "Gonna make you cry, baby, and everyone will know. Everyone."

God, it feels so good, your tongue and now your fingers, probing, opening me, teasing my clit with just the tip of your tongue and then moving away, pinching it between two fingers, the sensations building, the need rising. I want your cock there. I want you filling me, fixing me, making me whole. Yet, somehow, though you don't say it, I know that you want me to come first, that you won't stop until I come, won't fuck me until I come.

"No more secrets, darling, no more pretending."

You press two fingers into my pussy and then use your thumb to part the cheeks of my ass and tickle me there, exposing, exploring. I feel weak, find myself suddenly grateful for the support of my desk—"Gonna make you scream"—I hear my moans as if they belonged to someone else, some other woman's voice, some other woman's body being played so well, so masterfully, being stroked and suckled and teased and (deep breath) . . . fucked, *oh, thank you, God,* fucked as you stand and thrust your cock inside me, impaling me, making the head of it dance within the tight walls of my cunt.

"Squeeze me," you order, and I do, helplessly contracting on you, coming from the very first dull thrust inside me. Your cock throbs inside me, rocks back and forth as you pull out to the tip and then slam right back in.

"Squeeze . . ." you say again, wrapping one hand in my long brown hair and pulling my head back so that you can kiss my lips, kiss me softly while you fuck me fast, forcefully—just how you said, just how I need it.

"That's right, baby, keep it steady now"—as if you're talking to a pony, steady pace, keep the rhythm. I buck against your body, loving the feel of your open jeans on my naked thighs, your cool leather vest on my hot skin.

I moan louder, knowing that I'll be heard, but not caring, not giving any thought to the repercussions, calling your name out, "Oh, my god! Yes, please, Yes!" as I come on you, move with you, hit the stride and keep it, sliding up and down on your powerful cock, riding it, then moving away at your signal and getting down on my knees in front of you and licking my own come from your cock, lapping at the sweet drops that coat my lips, ignoring the pounding at my door.

Afterwards, we're warm and sticky, naked and sweaty, collapsed on the floor of my office with our clothes piled behind us for pillows. I lean up on one side to kiss you, to kiss your open mouth and taste myself, to let you taste yourself on my lips. I know that I can talk to you now, that something has changed inside me. Know that next time I will say, "I *need* your cock. Please, baby, please let me suck it, let me drink from you, devour you. I am so hungry . . ." say anything I want, anything at all.

"Did you open your gift yet?" you ask softly, stroking my hair away from my face, staring directly into my eyes.

"No. I was saving it." Imagining something like this, not as good as this, but the same freedom of it, the key that would unlock this door and let loose my soul.

But now, I realize the truth, that I don't need a key. Or, really, that I had the key the whole time, and only lacked the courage to turn it.

All Access

I have a friend who's a bouncer here; he showed me around. That's how I know where to go when I make it backstage. I pass down a narrow hallway packed with black-clad roadies and sleazy-looking rock journalists, plus a few groupies; they all look me over pointedly, not even caring that I can tell they're checking me out. It's what I expect, after all; I'm not wearing much. Just a tight pair of electric blue patent-leather hot pants, a skintight string bikini top with red flames on the tits, and knee-high logging boots. My black leather biker jacket's dangling from my hand. I took it off so I can show everything. The bikini top is so tight you can see my nipples through it, especially when they get all hard like this under the gaze of so many people.

As I squeeze down the hallway, I see the guys looking at me hungrily, openly, saying "Hi" and "Who are you?" and "Light my fire" and shit like that. The women, dressed kind of like me with their skimpy little fetishwear and their provocative tattoos, look at me nastily, viciously, knowing I'm the competition. All except for one. She's got short blonde hair and she's wearing a skintight pair of leather hip-huggers and a bikini top like mine, minus the flames. Her breasts are smaller than mine, but they're gorgeous. She looks at me, her eyes roving over my breasts, my belly, my legs. She doesn't seem to mind at all that I know she's looking. I smile at her. She smiles back, and as I pass, she reaches out and her fingertips graze my belly. Her touch feels electric.

At the end of the hallway I find a huge biker dude in leather. I show him my pass. All Access. He looks at it, his eyes narrowed. I feel my stomach churning. It's a pretty good forgery, but it's not *that* good.

He looks at my face, looks at my tits, hands me back the pass. He opens the door.

I'm deep backstage, now, back where the band hangs out. There's a long narrow hallway with several rooms on each side. I can hear some of them fucking around with their instruments. I glance into the rooms and recognize faces. Then I look up and stop dead in my tracks.

You're standing at the end of the corridor, in front of the door with a star on it. You're looking right at me.

Your eyes rove over my breasts, and my nipples stiffen fully under the tight top. God. You're looking at me. Your eyes travel over my stomach, over the form-fitting shorts, lingering for a long time on the way they hug my pussy, conforming to its folds. I look at you and feel dizzy. You're looking at my cunt.

You look at my face, smile at me. I'm too nervous to smile back.

You jerk your head slightly, toward the door with the star on it.

Then you open it and go through, leaving the door open.

I'm afraid my knees are going to give way. I feel wobbly as I hurry down the corridor after you, heading for the dressing room. I can feel the heat between my legs, from where you looked at me, igniting my cunt as if you have laser vision.

There are candles lit in the room, and I can smell incense. The lights are down low. There's a black leather couch. You're sitting on it, your legs spread, your tight leather pants showing your package, full and inviting.

Shaking, I walk over to you. I'm so nervous I forget to close the door, but you don't seem to care.

You pull me down onto you. The second my body touches

yours, I feel like I want to come. Your lips mold to mine, your tongue tasting of cigarettes and vodka as it enters me. I feel your hands pulling open the tie of my bikini top. It falls away easily, and your hands find my breasts.

I moan softly as you pinch my nipples; you're laying back on the couch, and I'm on top of you, my legs spread over your waist. As I settle down over you, I wriggle down farther, pressing my tightly-clad pussy to your crotch. I can feel the swell of your cock. I can feel it getting hard.

My mouth comes free from yours and I reach for your belt, panting. I've got to have it. I can't believe this is happening, but I've got to have you in my mouth.

When your cock comes free of your pants, it's just as big as I imagined. I feel my pussy pulsing hungrily as I breathe in your smell. I close my lips over the head of your cock and swirl my tongue around, tasting your pre-come. It tastes divine; it makes me want you even more. My lips travel down your shaft as I swallow you all. You run your fingers through my hair as you moan. I start sucking your cock, desperately wanting your come.

That's when I feel the second pair of hands, coming around my waist. Unbuttoning my skintight patent-leather shorts. Pulling the zipper down.

I look up from your cock, look over my shoulder. It's the girl from the hall. I see that she remembered to close the door.

Your hand in my hair guides me back down onto your cock as she peels the shorts away from my moist skin, discovering that I'm not wearing anything underneath. Nothing at all. I keep sucking your cock, wanting it more than ever. The shorts slide easily down my thighs, my calves, over my ankles. Her hand comes up between my legs and I feel her stroking my smooth pussy. I feel her fingers, two of them, sliding into me, making me gasp. She has short fingernails. She starts to fuck me.

That only makes me suck your cock harder, because it feels so fucking good. It's like she's fucked me for a million years; she knows everything about my pussy. Her fingertips go right to my G-spot and her other hand finds my clit, toying with the small ring. She gives me three fingers, all the way, up to the knuckles. She presses firmly on my spot and I moan. She works my clit and my whole body, naked now except for the boots, trembles with pleasure.

I look up at you, my eyes wide, taking in your gorgeous, familiar face as you watch me suck you. You're looking right at me, like you can't get enough of my face, you can't get enough of watching my mouth curve around your cock as my head bobs up and down.

She's fucking me faster, now, three fingers in rhythmically, hitting the right spot each time, the other hand working my clit. I'm going to come. I'm going to come with your cock in my mouth.

You come before I do, though, I guess because I'm sucking you so good, because I want your come so badly in my mouth. I swallow it all. Every drop. As she listens to you moan, she fucks me faster, hitting my G-spot harder, pressing more firmly on my clit. That's when I come, myself, feeling the thickness of your come filling my throat, its taste overwhelming me as I swallow. My whole naked body explodes in ecstasy, radiating out from my fucked-full cunt. I slump forward on top of you, her hand still inside me.

Her fingers slide out of me and you cradle my head between you and the back of the sofa. I feel helpless, just lost in the warmth of your embrace. You roll me over onto my back, so I'm kind of sitting in your lap, my legs stretching out to the end of the sofa. Your hands play with my breasts, making me whimper in pleasure as I watch her, the gorgeous, short-haired blonde girl with the small tits.

She's taking her clothes off.

The bikini top, and the pants, too. The pants are so tight she has to peel them, really work to get them off. She's not wearing anything underneath them, anything at all, just like me.

Naked, now, she saunters back to the sofa, looking into my eyes. I see what she wants, and I give it to her.

I slowly spread my legs.

She goes down onto her knees, her face descending between my thighs like she can't wait for it. And she doesn't; I let out a wild moan as I feel her tongue on my still-sensitive clit. She starts to eat me out.

You tip my head back and lean down, your mouth on mine again. You don't even care that I just sucked your cock, just swallowed your come. Your tongue delves deep into me and you keep playing with my breasts. My nipples are sensitive enough that it feels, as you pinch them, like there's a direct connection between her tongue on my clit and your hands on my tits. I'm going to come again. She eats me out mercilessly, devouring my pussy. Her fingers slide into me again as her tongue pulses on my clit. I'm going to come. And I do, writhing in your grasp, your tongue invading me and your hands controlling my breasts as she takes possession of my pussy again, takes it all, takes it and makes me come.

You're both on top of me, then, the two of you kissing, her small breasts dangling in my face. I take one nipple in my mouth and start to suckle her. She gasps and says "Mmmmm, you want it, huh? I had you figured for a straight girl..." and then she's reaching down behind me, to where your soft cock presses against my back. She curves her hand around it, starts to play with it.

Your cock starts to get hard.

I'm still lost in her breasts, loving the feel of the warm, smooth flesh against my face as I lick her nipples. You slip out from under me, your cock all the way hard, now, and she guides me down off the sofa, onto my knees, while she sits in front of me and spreads her legs.

She eases my face between her thighs, spreading her pussy lips for me. My lips press to hers and I taste the sharpness of her cunt, so wet it drips down onto my chin as I lick it. I lick deeper and she moans as I make my way up to her clit. I like the way it makes her moan. I close my lips over her clit and begin working my tongue, needing her. Needing her to come for me.

You've got me on my knees, now, leaning forward on the sofa between her spread legs. You've got my ass raised high in the air, your hands holding my hips in place. You're behind me, preparing to enter me.

I feel your cock against my pussy. I'm so wet even a cock as big as yours just slides right in. I gasp as it hits my deepest point, filling me. You groan a little, start fucking me. It feels incredible. It makes me want to eat her pussy even more. I delve into it with my desperate tongue, wanting more, more of her juice, more of her taste. Her clit is so big and firm and hard against the tip of my tongue. Her delicate hands brush gently through my hair. You reach over me and guide my hands up to her breasts, and I play with her nipples as you fuck me from behind. You take firm hold of my hips and start to give it to me hard, really hard, like you're getting ready to come. The sensations overwhelm me, the taste of her pussy, the feel of her breasts in my hands, her fingertips gently caressing my face, my nipples brushing against the rough leather of the sofa. It's too much. It's going to make me come again.

This time, I come first, moaning into her pussy as she closes her thighs around me. You don't slow down, pounding me as you get closer to your own orgasm. I keep licking her clit, never wanting to stop. And then, unexpected, she comes, her ass rising, her hips pumping, forcing her pussy against my face as the spasms wrack her body. That's when you let go, too, your cock pulsing inside me, and I feel the wetness flooding my pussy, fresh wetness, your second load of come inside me.

I lay there, slumped between the two of you, as I listen to your rhythmic breathing and her little whimpers of exhausted ecstasy. She reaches for a package on the nearby table and then extracts and lights a clove cigarette. The intense smoke smells sweet, overpowering the scent that covers my face. The scent of her pussy.

There's a knock on the door. Someone calls your name. "Show time," he says.

"Gotta go," you tell us, tucking your big, gorgeous cock away and zipping up your leather pants. You're going out there, onto the stage. You're going out there to play, with your cock still dripping my juice. A shiver goes through me.

I look up at her as you open the door and go away, leaving it wide open. I'm still kneeling on the floor, my ass in the air, my pussy feeling open and full from you. My eyes meet hers. Her pink lips smile around the butt of the clove.

She nods toward the door.

"Come on," she tells me. "Let's go watch the show."

Lights Out

I know I shouldn't sneak into your studio apartment. I know it's risky; I know it's wrong. I know I'm shameless, horrible, brazen, blatant, naughty. But I do it anyway, because I don't care. I've still got your key. No problem at all for me to be stealthy and slide inside.

The lights are out. The room's cold; I can sense a window open somewhere behind a dark curtain. I feel my nipples stiffen, feel the breeze on my thighs. I wait there for my eyes to adjust to the darkness, but the curtains are pulled and it's almost black. Finally, I inch across the room breathing slowly and deeply, my heart pounding. Are you there? I listen for your breathing, but all I can hear is the throbbing of my own pulse in my ears. I feel my knee hit the bed. I lean over, reaching out for you.

The bed is empty. The sheets have been turned down, but you're not there.

I wonder where you are. Vanished, when I expected you here, when my whole plan was to surprise you. I should go, I tell myself, but there's no chance of that. No chance at all.

Instead, I reach up and unzip my dress.

I'm not wearing much at all underneath it, and the skimpy thong joins my dress in a rumpled ball next to the bed. I kick off my shoes. Nude, I shiver with the cold. I want to close the window, but I can't bear to change a thing.

I crawl into the bed. My body slides easily between the cold satin sheets. The smooth material excites every inch of my naked body. I feel my nipples stiffening still more, almost painfully. Casually, I slide my hand between my legs, touch my pussy. I'm wet—intensely wet, and I moan softly as my fingers probe my entrance.

I aimlessly stroke my pussy, feeling it moistening even further. I spread my legs wide and savor the satin sheets as they rub my thighs, my calves, my feet. I let my hand laze over my breasts and gently pinch my nipples. I lay there thinking of you, thinking about what I'm doing. How wrong it is. How naughty it is. How I shouldn't be doing it, and how I'm doing it anyway. How I *want* to do it. I think about all the things I want to do, and I stroke my pussy more, feeling its heat.

Will you enter the room alone? Discover me in your bed and order me out? There are so many reasons why I shouldn't be here—why we're bad for each other. Connecting with you again will set us back, won't it? Or maybe it will simply be one more time for old time's sake.

Will you join me? Will you come in with someone else—with several someones, or many? Will one more be all right? I feel my pussy pulsing as I envision all the possible scenarios, as the flesh of my body tingles in anticipation of your touch. I hear your key in the lock outside. The door opens, and you're silhouetted in a rectangle of light. You're alone.

The sight of you makes me hurt. My whole body aches for you.

You don't see me. You close the door behind you. I hold my breath and listen to your footsteps as you cross the room, draw back the curtain. I see your back, illuminated by a single shaft of moonlight over your shoulder. You shut the window, and it makes a hollow thud as it slams. You draw the curtains and again you're hidden from me, floating somewhere in utter darkness as my soul reaches for you, my legs spread and wanting you between them.

I hear the ruffle of clothes as you start to undress in the darkness.

My head spins as I listen to your clothing hitting the floor, listen to your breathing. I slowly inch my legs together, turning on my side. Can you hear me moving? Can you hear my breath, pained and tight with the excitement of being this close to you, here, in your bed?

Then I feel the sheets pulled back, and your body slides between them. Against mine. Hot, your flesh burning me. Your hands finding my waist, your leg, soft with hair, coming up easily between my smooth thighs.

Do you know it's me? Do you know I've been waiting for you? Or do you not care who it is?

I feel your hand on my breast, your thumb pressing my swollen nipple. Your lips find mine in the darkness, flawlessly, without searching. Your mouth forces mine open and I feel your tongue plunging into me.

Your body shifts and you push against me, forcing me onto my back. I gasp as I feel your weight between my legs, your knee hard against my pussy, against my clit. Now both your hands are on my breasts, pinching my nipples carelessly, taking no time to explore my breasts, taking no time to see how much pressure I can take. Your tongue burrows into my mouth, taking me, and I inhale deeply of your scent—intense, male, overpowering. Dominant.

Fear seizes me as both your legs slide easily between mine. What if it's not you? Your smell is so unfamiliar, so intoxicating, I could be making love with a stranger. I *am* making love with a stranger. It could be you, a burglar, a killer. I feel a surge go through my pussy as your knees spread my legs forcibly and I feel myself lifting my ass off the satin sheets to meet you.

You pinch my nipples harder as your cock finds my entrance. I'm so wet there's no hand needed to guide you in, and mine rest useless at my sides. I'm under your control, desperate to be taken by you.

I feel the first thrust going through me, sending a shudder of excitement and fear into my very soul. I can't believe how wet I am. My pussy is so sensitive I feel every inch of your thrust, my body conforming to the shape of your cock. Is it familiar? Is the shape what I expect? Is it your cock? A stranger's cock?

My ass lifts high off the bed, meeting you as you come down into me, as deep as you can go. I'm ready to come, already. Your lips leave mine and I can smell your breath, sweet and exhilarating, your lips hovering above me as you thrust into me. I come, my throat tightening and my gasp coming, strangled, the orgasm unexpected as it explodes through me. "Oh God," I whisper, and I want to add "what have I done," but I know. I know what I've done. I throw my arms around you and pull you close, my thighs closing tight around your hips. You're heavy, and as you pound down into me my legs are forced wider, making me expose myself. My hands move down your back to find your ass, its muscles clenching as you thrust. You kiss me again, and your tongue plunges into me as deeply as your cock.

"Oh God," I whisper. "Oh God, I'm going to....again....I'm going to..." and then I do, embarrassed that you've made me come so hard, so fast, that I'm so completely under your control, that you own me. I open wider to you, and I feel you pull out, kneeling back away from me.

I know what you want, somehow, instinctively. I'm on you in an instant, my lower body pressed against the satin sheets, my upper body propped up on one arm while the other finds your cock and guides it to my mouth. I taste so strong on your cock, but what I want is to taste you. I take your cock deep, feeling it at the back of my throat, swallowing. My head moves smoothly up and down as I breathe deeply, smelling you and me mingled with every thrust of your cock into me. Hungrily, I devour you.

When you pull me off of your cock, I'm panting, moaning softly, I whisper "Please....please....please...."

But you gently take hold of my shoulders, turning me around. Now I know what you want, again, and I want it, too, more than anything. You guide me onto my hands and knees and I lift my behind as high as it will go into the air, presenting it to you.

You enter me with a single smooth thrust, your cock slippery, my pussy drenched and begging for you. I gasp as it goes in, and I strain back against you, pushing myself onto you. Your strong hands rest on my ass. My hips wriggle desperately, trying to force you deeper. I can feel the head of your cock thick and firm as deep in me as it can go. I moan softly as you pull back and begin to fuck me.

I can't believe I'm going to come again—so fast, so quick, a third time. So effortlessly. You lean back and hold still while I push myself onto you, desperately fucking my body onto your cock, impaling myself. I come, gasping, my body flushing as I accept that you know how bad I want you, that I can't stop my body from shoving itself onto your cock. You seem to sense the moment of my orgasm, and that's when you begin fucking me again. Hard, this time, mercilessly—now, for your own orgasm.

But there's one way left you want to have me, and I could no more say no than I could fly to the moon. When I feel your cockhead opening the entrance of my pussy as it slips out, I know what to expect, and despite the faint wave of fear that goes through me, I want it. I want it more than anything.

I feel the head of your cock between my cheeks, your thumbs gently parting them as you seek my rear entrance. I hold still, frightened but longing for it. I feel the cold drizzle between my cheeks, feel the head of your cock rubbing up and down in the small space. Then you push in.

I gasp the first time, unable to accept it. My naked body trembles and you push, gently but firmly, again.

Again, my back door clenches, unwilling. Not nearly as desperate for your cock as I am.

Another cold drizzle, making me shut my eyes, tight. Again your cock, swirling in tiny circles at my entrance. Again, the thickness of your head, parting my cheeks, this time, insistent.

When it slips in I gasp, disbelieving. My muscles clench quickly, holding your cock as tightly as they can. You hold still, then take firm hold of my hips I feel you pulling me back onto you.

I accept you all, every way you want to take me. My mouth opens in a soundless moan. You hold motionless, as I feel my muscles tightening....then relaxing around you. Your hands hold my hips, tightly and I ache with hunger to have your cock in me, as deep as it will go. But you hold still, feeling my body adapt to the shape and size of your cock.

I want it. I want it more than I've ever wanted anything.

I want to offer it to you. I want to give you this gift.

Slowly, I lower my upper body down onto my shoulders, my breasts pressing firm against the damp satin sheets. I reach back with my hands. My fingertips creep over yours, continue down to my ass.

Desperately, a moaning supplicant, I part my cheeks as far as they will go.

Your own fingers tighten, merciless. You pull me onto you with force.

I taste the pillow slick and salty against my tongue as you guide me back onto your cock, forcing it into my ass. I hold my cheeks wide as you take me. I bite the pillow, shivering, overwhelmed by the sudden rush of pleasure. I whisper "Oh, yes," but I know you can't hear me with my face pressed into the pillow like that. Which I prefer, because

I flush with sudden shame; I feel my face getting hot as I accept how good it feels. How much, how hard, I want it.

You guide me back, your cock sliding easily out of me, halfway, three-quarters—and then you pull me back onto you, wrenching a moan out of me this time, an uncontrollable moan that I can't stifle.

Three more thrusts guided by you, pulled by you onto your cock, and I lose control. My hands come away from my buttocks and grab the pillow, hard, wrenching, my teeth still closed around it. I hear the pillowcase rupturing, a high-pitched tear in the darkness mingling with my moans. I grasp the headboard fiercely, gripping it because I no longer need to spread my cheeks to tell you how much I want it in my ass. I no longer need to do that because I'm moaning softly "Fuck me....fuck me....fuck me...." as I smell the dusty down. "Fuck me....fuck me....fuck me...." The words come out in tiny sobs, as I desperately beg for you to take me as deeply as I need to be taken. But I'm the one whose hips are driving me back onto you, whose hands are gripping the headboard, whose whole body tightens with effort as I strain to fuck myself harder onto your cock. And then, sobbing openly now, not believing it's happening, not believing it *can* happen, I come—harder than I have ever come, my pussy tightening, empty as my ass fills with your sudden thrusts, as the contraction of my muscles invites you in, invites you to fuck me. Just fuck me.

You push forward, forcing me off my knees and up against the headboard, my body twisted improbably, my hands still grasping the headboard as my breasts push against the satin pillow. You push forward hard, forcing my lower body against the mattress, grinding your hips against my behind, ravishing my asshole with your cock. Now it's you who are taking me. My naked body still pulses in orgasm, the sensations overwhelming me as you pound into my asshole. Every erogenous zone I have is alive, on fire, as you possess my most private entrance and make me come, harder, continuously, as I sob and shriek and moan under your relentlessly driving body. Then, in a moment of explosive surrender, I realize you're about to come and I open for you, relinquishing the intensity of my own orgasm to feel your cock pulse inside me. You groan behind me, in the dark, your sweat scattering across my back and ass in a fine mist as you plunge into me in three fierce, short, violent thrusts, the sensitized muscles of my anus so tight around your cock that I can feel the hot sensation as you fill me.

Are they tears or sweat, moistening my cheeks? My whole body crawls with droplets, every inch of my flesh alive. With a desperate, untamed shudder, you give me your last, and your weight atop me makes me hot—suddenly, uncontrollably dripping. Underneath me, the satin sheets grow wet; they're soaked now, and I can feel a spreading patch between my legs where my empty, longing pussy wept for your cock as you took my ass.

I feel your breath hot on the back of my neck, but you don't kiss it. You don't kiss my shoulder, don't rise from me to let me turn over. All I can do is lay immobile, vulnerable and helpless underneath you, wanting more of you, feeling hungry for it as your softening cock slips out of my ass.

When I feel your weight rise off of me, I know better than to speak a word. I lay there and listen to you dress, inhaling deeply as if these are the last breaths of your fleeting scent that I will ever have. Your footsteps are heavy as you walk to the door. You pause, just for a moment, and with my eyes shut tight I don't know if you are looking back at me. But I like to think so.

I slide off the bed, my legs unsteady. On my hands and knees, I grope for my dress. I find it balled just under the bed, twisted and inside-out. I pull it right-side-out and ineptly seek the neck hole several times before I can find it. Still on my knees, I start to put it on. My body is slippery as I pull the dress over my head. I'm dripping with sweat and can feel your come thinning with my body heat, slowly leaking onto my thighs. I fancy that I hear a steady stream of drops against the carpet.

The silk dress slides down my moistened body, soaking itself with my sweat as it embraces me. I don't bother with the panties. I take hold of my shoes and, dragging them behind me by the straps, like recalcitrant puppies on leashes, I crawl to the door. I feel dizzy as I rise. I have to lean against the doorknob, hard, for several minutes before I have the strength even to turn it.

I open the door, squinting into the light. I stand there and turn, looking back at the bed we've so thoroughly ruined.

I see nothing. I am staring into darkness.

I take a deep breath. I can smell you, and I can smell me. Your come is the strongest scent, but my pussy wrestles it for dominance in the small, now hot room. Your sweat, my sweat, and the lingering aroma of your aftershave send shivers through my body, and I feel the slickness awkwardly descending the backs of my thighs.

I look into the black, knowing the bed is there, somewhere, its sheets soaked, its covers tangled, its pillowcases gnawed through by my teeth.

The door makes a hollow thud as I close it.

On the House

Nadine has been my friend since high school, but unlike so many of the kids I grew up with, she hasn't changed in all the years I've known her. Most of my buddies have matured, which I guess could be expected. Time marches on, right? Unfortunately, with maturity seems to have come indescribable boredom. I barely recognize the pranksters and partiers from my youth, and dinners and cocktail hours with them can be more numbing than Xanax.

Nadine's different. She always wants to push the limits just like she did back in tenth grade. She is never satisfied with a calm evening out, which I find part terrifying and part thrilling. Bar-hopping with her is always an adventure. Sometimes we have a blast. We make up fake names and phony backgrounds and share them with strangers. We go dancing at clubs where nobody knows us and join in on amateur nights. I can handle getting crazy with her occasionally. Every once and awhile everyone needs to blow off a little extra energy. But other times, she goes beyond my boundaries. Way beyond. Then, even though we're together, she's on her own.

Tonight, she has the insane idea that we will get guys to buy us drinks. It's her verbally stated mission that we don't put our money on the table all night long, but that we both end up plenty lubricated. I'm not up with this. Or down with this. It seems too calculated to be any fun. If a guy wants to buy me a brew, then let him come to that decision himself. But I don't want to be a cocktease for a Cosmopolitan. I'm worth more than that. Still, I watch my pretty friend go into overdrive, batting her lush eyelashes at a rowdy college-aged foursome nearby. What's she going to do? Bang them all for a beer?

When she makes noises about being included in their next round, they ask sweetly if she's the one buying, and she stalks off across the room in a huff, visibly angered by their echoing laughter. At precisely this moment, a shot of golden tequila suddenly appears on the bar in front of me like magic.

"I didn't order this," I tell you.

"On the house," you say, dark eyes smiling at me.

"But I wasn't—"

"—in on the game," you nod, completing the thought. "I know. I heard your friend talking to you."

When I raise my eyebrows, you continue with a shrug.

"Bartenders have a knack for eavesdropping. So I heard all about the plan, and then I stayed back here and watched her make a complete fool of herself. Gold-diggers like her come in every evening. You didn't need to go that route, and that's why I wanted to buy you a drink."

"Buy—" I say, and now I *am* flirting, because I like the way you're looking at me. Your expression makes me feel girlish and giggly, and I'm getting into the mood of being in a bar and bantering. This is what Nadine wanted from the get-go, but she pursued it too hard and ended up solo. I see her from the corner of my eye. She's leaning up against the jukebox, pretending that she's busy selecting, but really showing off her body to whoever might be looking. I can tell from the way that she arches her back and tosses her hair that she's working an imaginary audience.

"So I don't actually 'buy' it," you say, "just one of the perks. But I get to choose who to spend my freebies on."

Now, I wait for you to come closer to me, and I lift my shot just as you reach for the wedge of neon-bright lime and the glass shaker of salt. You squeeze lime juice onto the back of your hand, and sprinkle on a snow flurry of salt and then wait to see what I'll do next. It's a silent dare, issued only with your dark eyes, but I'm more than up for the challenge. I swallow hard, then lean forward and lick the back of your hand clean, and then I lean even closer, and I move quickly to bring my lips to yours.

This clinch with a stranger comes as a total a surprise to Nadine, who has returned from her sulky sojourn to the jukebox just in time to catch our liplock. Never one to be at a loss for words, she sums up the situation in a single sentence. "You licking bartenders now?" she sneers at me. "Well, I guess that's one surefire way to get drinks for free."

"Not for free," I explain, looking at her with narrowed eyes. "We're making a trade—"

You shake your head at Nadine, and I can tell that your opinion of her is even lower now than it was at the start of the evening. Then you shrug, and I watch you whisper something to your pert blonde co-worker, and then motion for me to follow you to the back room, behind the scenes of this trendy watering hole. Nadine says, "Hey," to me, as if that's going to keep me on the bar stool.

This time, I'm the one to shrug at her, and I slide off and walk after you, through the swinging back door. But we don't stop there, back in the stock room with the boxes of supplies. We keep on going. All the way up the stairs that take us to the roof. Now, we're literally on top of the "house," and I come into your arms, not caring that I don't know your name. Not concerned with anything except your strong arms tight around me, lifting me up, and your body warm and hard beneath my own.

From the rooftop of this Santa Monica bar, we can hear the ocean and smell the crisp salt in the air. That scent reminds me of licking the salt off your skin, and it makes me even more excited. On the street below, cars cruise endlessly in search of parking spaces. This is a ritzy neighborhood filled with many places where people want to go.

But I only want to go higher into your arms. I only want to feel your skin on mine. Nadine had an agenda tonight. I didn't until I met you. Thankfully, your plans seem to mimic my own. You know exactly how to take control. Raising me upwards and holding me tightly. Then slipping me down for a moment so that you can reach under my short lace-hemmed skirt and run your fingers along the waistband of my pale blue satin panties. They're lovely, this set. An innocent sky blue trimmed with the same sort of lace that scallops the edge of my skirt. You pull the panties down with a quick gesture, and I step out of them, then wait to see what you're going to do next.

Without a word, you bend me over the edge of the roof. I hold my breath for a moment, waiting for the first taste of your cock inside me. But you don't rush. You bend down on the gravel and bring your mouth to the split of my body. You lick between my legs from behind, and I exhale in a rush at that sensation. You could make me come with a few rotations of your tongue. I'm that excited to be up here, doing something so unique for someone as proper as I am.

You don't want me to come on your mouth, though. You want me to ride you, and you get into position and then slide into me from behind so that I can look out at the moving city while feeling your moving body on mine. I can't remember ever being so at ease while having sex. A calmness steals through me as I stare out at the people wandering down below, at the seaside vision between two tall condominiums across the way. The black water sheens silver when the moonlight hits it. I gaze out at that million-dollar view as your fingers come into play. You stroke up along my waist and up to my breasts, and you tweak my nipples through the light fabric of my semi-sheer blouse. Then down your hands go again, until you're pulling my skirt up in front. You want to touch my pussy while you fuck me, and I squirm in your arms to get myself into the best position for that. I want to feel your strong fingers against my clit, want you to spread me open, spread me wide, and help me reach the end.

We're in perfect synchronicity as we fuck. There are no words, which is fine because we don't need to talk. I need only your rock-hard rod inside me, and the view before me, and your fingertips sparkling soft against my clit. I close my eyes for one moment as the pleasure waves through me, and then open them up just in time to see Nadine down there below us, walking to some stranger's car on the boulevard. She doesn't look up once, doesn't think for a minute that I'd be up here doing this with you.

I know that you see her, too, and we both watch as she climbs into the back seat of the SUV with one of the rowdy foursome from the bar.

"Giving head for a beer," you murmur to me as I come.

"While I get mine on the house," I laugh, turning in your embrace to the sound of crashing waves.

A Loose Interpretation

They flee from me that sometime did me seek,
With naked foot stalking in my chamber.

The phone rings at 1:33 a.m., tearing me from sleep. I fumble for the receiver, knocking over a stack of books on my nightstand. In that haze between sleep and wakefulness, I finally find the phone beneath a 49ers T-shirt and mumble something that almost sounds like hello.

"I know what you want." Your whisper in darkness over the telephone line has me fully awake in a heartbeat, yet I don't respond. I'm sure if I remain quiet, you'll keep right on talking. "I know what you need." The urgency in your deep voice makes me tremble. I clutch the receiver so tightly that the muscles in my hand begin to cramp. "You're a bad girl, aren't you?"

I can't answer. Not yet. But my breathing, heavy, frightened, tells you that I understand.

"Be over here in twenty minutes," you say, "wear a dress without panties, put your hair in a ponytail, and be natural. No make-up. Got it?"

I nod, although I know full well that you can't see me, and then I manage to choke out, "Yeah, okay. I'll be there."

"Good."

I hang up the phone and look at the digital clock on the nightstand. 1:35. I get out of bed, flick on the overhead light, and stand naked in front of the mirror on the back of my closet, checking myself out. I run my fingertips lightly over my slim body, cupping my small, firm breasts, circling my waist. After a moment, I move even closer to my reflection, pushing back my birch-blonde hair with one hand and observing my image with the calculated look of a beauty pageant judge: high cheekbones, large green eyes, pouty lips.

I can hear your voice in my head, complimenting me, and I turn in front of the mirror and look at myself over one shoulder, an approving smile touching the corners of my mouth. I have slender hips, but a round buoyant ass.

I can imagine you admiring my curves, the contours of my muscles, the sleek lines of the bones beneath my skin. Seeing myself through your eyes, I lift my right hand and spank myself once, hard, watching intently as the purple-outlined print appears on my ass like a brand.

Ten minutes late will be ten strokes.

I open the closet and regard my wardrobe for a moment before choosing a prim pale blue sundress with a lace collar. It's something a librarian would feel comfortable wearing, something left-over from when I was a different sort of girl. The severe style makes my lack of underclothes all the more sexy, and the color of the fabric brings a glow to my eyes, a feverish light.

I twist my silvery curls into a loose knot and capture the 'do' with a tortoise-shell barrette. Then I grab my wallet and car keys, turn out the light, and hurry out the door.

I have seen them gentle, tame and meek
That now are wild and do not remember
That sometime they put themself in danger
To take bread at my hand, and now they range
Busily seeking with a continual change...

I picture you waiting for me. You're kicked back on your worn leather sofa, watching an old Bogart film on TV. Every so often you look at the clock, judging the time. Then you gaze back at the television, watching Bogie light a cigarette before glancing back at the clock.

It's easy for me to picture your every move. At 1:59 you'll realize that I'm playing with you. You'll rub one hand over your whiskers, starting to show now even though you shaved after work. You think about the way your beard will feel against my skin when you kiss me.

2:02. I'm in for it now, and that thought makes you harder than hard. We both know full well that the drive to your place takes me ten minutes. But here I am, a full seven minutes late. You'll have my pretty bottom over your lap the instant I walk through the door. I know that. I know all about that. You'll give me a good, thorough spanking, one that will warm my ass and heat my pussy.

2:04 Now, I'm testing you.

And we both know it.

Thanked be fortune, it hath been otherwise
Twenty times better, but once in special.

I sit in my car, one block from your apartment, watching the numbers change on the dashboard clock. I know that you'll be angry enough to give me exactly what I need, just like you promised over the phone. Penance. I shift around in the bucket seat, growing more excited, and especially aware of the wetness because I'm not wearing underpants.

Ten minutes late will be ten strokes.

Maybe you'll use your belt. God, I want it so badly, to be punished, to be overwhelmed. My heart races as I start the ignition and drive down the street, pulling into your driveway and cutting the engine. Then, trembling slightly, I get out of the car and walk to your studio. I haven't even knocked on the door when you open it, and you grab me high up on the arm and drag me into the room.

"Naughty girl," you say. I can hear the smile in your voice, but that doesn't make you any less severe. In fact, you look particularly stern this evening. Your thick, black hair is combed back off your forehead, and your normally soft brown eyes regard me coldly. "You're in for it," you hiss, gripping onto me even more tightly. "You're due for a proper hiding."

To me, this sounds more like a sexy promise than any sort of threat. Still, I know better than to speak, and I wait silently for your command. Will you do it to me on the sofa or take me into the bedroom?

"Put your hands flat against the wall," you order, surprising me. I turn my back to you and place my palms on the smooth, cool wall, supporting myself. You set one hand firmly in the small of my back, causing me to arch forward, to offer my ass to you like a wonderful gift. You slowly lift my dress, dragging the material along my thighs, taking your time to unveil my body. You gather the fabric high up on my waist, so that the blue silk falls to either side, framing me.

"Ten minutes late," you say softly, close to my ear.

I nod.

"Ten."

I nod again.

"Bend over further."

I lower my hands on the wall, arching even higher for you, feeling deliciously exposed. You go down on your knees behind me and you bury your face in the split of my body, drinking in my heady scent. You hold me open from behind and lick the drops of my honey that have already dampened my inner thighs.

You use your thumbs to further spread the lips of my pussy, and then without warning, you thrust your tongue deep inside me, making me moan and buck against you. You swirl your tongue in dangerous circles, then pull back and slide two fingers inside me. Now, my muscles start to contract, letting you know how close I am to coming. But before I'm able to climax, you withdraw your fingers and stand up. Gently, you take one of my hands and place it where it will give me the most pleasure.

"Touch yourself," you order. "Like you do when you're in bed alone, thinking of all the things you want me to do with you. Or to you."

I blush that you've read my secrets so well, but I do just as I'm told, caressing myself, slipping my fingers over and around my pulsing clit.

"I want you to keep touching yourself while I punish you," you tell me. "Understand?"

I nod.

"I can't hear you."

"Yes, Sir."

"Better."

You pull your belt free from the loops of your jeans, staring as I undulate my hips, continuing the rhythm that you've set with your tongue and fingers. You suck in your breath, watching me. It's like I'm your own personal sex show—I can feel that. I'm putting on a performance and you're getting hot. My head dips down and my eyes close. I am already breathing hard, my fingers increasing their speed, faster and faster now, hips sliding back and forth, head dropping further forward, back muscles tensed, entire body poised on the brink.

For one instant, you give in to me, pressing forward so I can feel your hard cock against my ass. But then you back up again. We have unfinished business.

Ten minutes means ten strokes.

You double the heavy leather belt in your hand and stand back from me to give yourself room. After a moment's hesitation, you tell me to take my dress all the way off. I do as you say, pausing to kiss you quickly before returning to my set position.

In thin array, after a pleasant guise,
When her loose gown from her shoulders did fall
And she caught me in her arms long and small;
Therewith all sweetly did me kiss,
And softly said, "Dear heart, how like you this?"

Just kissing you makes me want more, makes me want you to be inside my mouth, to feel my lips around your throbbing cock, suckling you, devouring you. Feeding from you.

"Ten," you say again, and I shift my weight nervously from one foot to the other. Anticipation beats inside of me. But then we're starting, and you swing and connect, once, twice, three times. I bow my head toward my chest, but I don't make a sound, nor do I stop caressing myself. In my mind, I hear your voice again, as you sounded on the phone: "I know what you want. I know what you need."

Four. Five. Six.

It was no dream; I lay broad waking.
But all is turned through my gentleness
Into a strange fashion of forsaking;

Seven. Eight. Nine.

Now, I let out a low moan. Tears spill freely from my eyes, and even though you can't see them, I'm sure that you know that I'm crying, know that I've been silently crying since you first made me take off the dress. You know everything there is to know about me.

You always have.

"People think you're such a good girl," you say quietly

to me, stroking my hot ass with one hand. "But we both know what you really are."

And I have leave to go of her goodness,
And she also to use newfangleness.

Ten.

With the last stroke, you give in. You rip your fly open and free your cock. I can sense just how turned on you are, because I know everything about you, as well. Without a word, you grab me around the waist and force me back onto you, force the entire length of your cock inside me with one long, powerful thrust. I come almost as soon as you enter me, keep on coming as you pound into me. I lean forward again, hands on the wall, while you hold onto my hips and fuck me with everything you have. It's as if you're still disciplining me, using the rod of your cock to more thoroughly punish me.

I'm crying and laughing at the same time, lost in how good it all feels, how whole I feel with you inside. You hold me even tighter for the last part of the wild ride, bucking with me, pulling me hard against you. Then, lifting me completely off the ground, you kiss me, your lips sliding in the downy softness of the nape of my neck. You come in a series of shattering explosions, and then, still holding me, still inside of me, you carry me to the sofa where we collapse together. Damp, exhausted, and satisfied.

But since that I so kindly am served
I would fain know what she hath deserved.

"You give me what I need," I whisper.

"I give you what you deserve," you respond, and I nod in answer, unable after all of it to speak.

Playing Possum

You're sleeping when I get home. I'm horny as hell, but I tell myself I won't wake you up. That would be inconsiderate. I strip off my clothes, noticing how the sweat dampens them, how my underwear is soaked. Those long drives home always get me worked up, ever since the radio broke: nothing to do but think about sex, especially about you. You and your cock.

I pull out the burgundy satin pajamas I like to sleep in. The smooth material ignites my flesh as I slip into it; I can feel its softness against my nipples, against my butt, against my thighs. Yawning, I move toward the bed. Then I see the light on the electric blanket. Damn it. You always want to sleep with that thing on. I usually talk you out of it, offering my body as a radiator, hot-blooded as I am. I wrap around you and you're toasty warm for the whole night, invariably—and I'm kept cool by the chill of your flesh. One of the benefits of having a lover with a wonky internal thermostat. Whenever you sleep alone, though, you crank that stupid electric blanket up all the way.

Normally, I have to sleep in clothes. You prefer sleeping naked, but I can't stand it. The only thing I like to do naked in bed is fuck. But there is no way I'm crawling in there dressed when you've had the blanket on. If I do, I'll wake up in an hour bathed in sodden satin.

I take off my pajamas and turn off the blanket, then crawl under the covers. It's stifling in here. I stretch out on the far side of the bed to get away from your body heat, but you've moved over to the middle, as usual, trying to take over my side. I finally give up and wrap myself around you, feeling your naked body against mine.

I feel it, against my arm. I don't mean to reach for you, it just brushes me. And then I can't let go.

Your cock is hard.

I say your name, a question, asking if you're awake.

You don't even grunt.

It's one of those things boys do, I know. You get hard throughout the night. I've woken up with your erection pressing against my ass, thinking you were getting frisky, while in reality you're still locked in a dream about ice cream sundaes or something. Normally, I ignore your midnight arousals. But now, after the long drive with me fantasizing about this cock in my hand, the touch of it makes me ignite.

I'm already slick with sweat. But I'm afraid you'll wake up with a start if I pull back the covers, so I brave the oppressive heat and get all the way under them.

God, your cock tastes good in my mouth.

I start sucking it hungrily, wanting more of you. I don't even care if you wake up; I just want your cock, your come. I can feel my pussy moistening with the taste of your flesh, of the tiny bead of pre-come that leaks out your tip and into my mouth. I reach up and run my hands over your chest, feeling your nipples, soft and small with the heat. I lick your cock all over, half expecting you to wake up.

But you don't, and I can feel my pussy throbbing with every thrust I give your cock, with every stroke my tongue lavishes on you.

I've got to have it.

I crawl on top of you, spreading my legs around your hips. You're hard, really hard, and your cock feels sticky from my mouth. I'm dripping sweat on top of you. Normally being hot makes me want to lay there and complain. But tonight it's making me want to fuck. Since I never get in bed naked unless I'm ready to fuck, there's little I can do to control myself.

I slide my cunt up the shaft of your cock, fit its head into me. I push myself down onto you, moaning softly as I take it. God, it feels incredible.

I start to fuck you. I can't tell if you're awake, and I don't even care anymore. I just want to fuck you until I come. I pump myself onto you, feeling your cock hit the right spot. I reach down between us and start rubbing my clit.

I say your name, just as a matter of politeness. But you don't respond; maybe you're still asleep. You always were such a deep sleeper.

I fuck you luxuriously for long minutes, savoring every stroke of my pussy down onto your cock. I kiss your chest and inhale your smell, letting it make me want you more. The feel of my naked body against yours excites me and makes me want to fuck you harder. But I go gentle, half of me not wanting to be rude and wake you up, the other half wanting to take as long as I can before I come, enjoying a slow, comfortable screw as I build up to my release.

But my release is coming quickly, the heat and our nakedness making it tumble on me almost unexpected. I twist and writhe as I come on top of you, pumping slowly and demandingly onto your cock.

I say your name as I come, but you don't respond. Asleep?

Then I feel you sitting up, as if you're awaking with a start. Or are you? Your arms go around me and you flip me easily, your cock never leaving my pussy. You shove me back and the covers go flying onto the ground. Reversing our positions, you push me onto my back so my head hangs over the foot of the bed. Then you start to fuck me. Hard, mercilessly.

I certainly don't think I'm going to come again, not so fast. But something about the surprise, about being taken like this when I thought you were asleep, when I thought I was just using you for my own pleasure, catches me totally off guard. I come, intensely, loud moans coming unbidden to my lips as you pound into me, fucking me hard with your eyes wide open, staring into mine.

Then I feel your thrusts quickening as you approach your own climax. When you come, it's loud, you shouting at the top of your lungs as if you're trying to wake the neighbors. I feel my pussy moisten with your come, and your thrusts intensify, then slack off as you finish your orgasm. You go limp, sliding off of me and laying on your side, your body against mine. Your eyes have fluttered closed. Your breathing is regular.

I say your name.

You don't respond.

Asleep?

I can't be sure, but I think I see the corner of your mouth twitching upward in the faintest hint of a smile.

Then again, maybe you're just playing possum.

I smile back, reach out for your cock, wet and dripping from my pussy, softening quickly now that you're spent. A drizzle of come leaks from the head. I wrap my hand around your soft cock.

"Pleasant dreams," I whisper, and slide down to suck it.

Front Row, Center

Sure, I'd heard of girls seducing their professors. Come on. Who hasn't? It's almost an urban legend, in fact, leggy redheads stalking fiercely down the halls of the English department, searching out the professor who could give them an A in exchange for a little T&A.

Truly, I must admit that I always thought the idea was nonsense. Or, if the stories *were* true, and a girl stooped that low for a higher GPA, she must have something wrong with her. Maybe people cheat in high school, because it's so boring. But college is supposed to be a place of almost-adults, right? Who are you really cheating but yourself? I know it sounds sappy now, but that's what I thought. And then I met you.

All right, I'll admit that I had dirty thoughts before our first class. See, there was a buzz. I heard about you before I saw you.

"Did you see the new Shakespeare prof?" I heard one coed whisper in the hall.

"I know," her friend said. "I can't believe I'm actually paying attention at an 8:00 class."

To clear my name ahead of time, let me explain that I'm a straight-A student. I don't need to fuck anyone to keep my grade point average where it should be. That's not my agenda in the slightest. But that doesn't stop me from having reservations about what I did. There's a strict policy at our college—teachers and students are not allowed to fraternize. A polite way to say: Do not fuck the student body. *Any* student body. Even one as pretty as mine.

I will also add that I don't normally break rules. I don't

jaywalk. I don't shoplift. I don't even steal grapes at the grocery store. I am honest to a fault. In the past, however, I didn't think it *was* a fault. That's how I've always been. Until... you became the new head of the Shakespeare department. Until I took your class and saw you in action, playing the roles of Hamlet, of Macbeth, of Iago with the ease of an actor from the Royal Shakespeare Company. You were mesmerizing. You didn't lecture us, but you taught. Five hundred students sat in total, awed silence for each hour and a half period.

On Tuesdays and Thursdays, I got to campus early. I never varied my spot in your class, seating myself front row, center, every time. But despite my best efforts, you didn't appear to take any extra notice of me. My tests came back with As, as usual, but no comments. Yet every so often I thought I saw a gleam in your eyes when you looked my way, the same longing I felt for you mirrored back at me.

This is why I left the note in your box. I can't explain it away. I wrote "Dear Professor, Being your slave, what should I do but tend upon the hours and times of your desire? I have no precious time at all to spend, nor services to do till you require..." and I continued through the entire Shakespeare sonnet, signing the letter, "Front Row, Center. Long, Dark Hair."

Then I waited.

The day after our term ended, I got a note requesting that I meet you during your office hours. I dressed impeccably in my normal collegiate manner, pressed jeans, stark white shirt, cardigan, penny loafers. Underneath, however, I wore the one lace panty set I own, a little black number bought a year ago on a whim.

I was on time to your office, as you must have expected, and when I knocked on the door you called for me to enter. I stood just inside the room, waiting for the next instruction. I didn't have to wait long. You walked over to me, ran your hands through my rich, mahogany hair, lifted my head toward yours, and kissed me.

Shivers ran through my body. I gripped onto you as if to keep from falling. You said, "I've noticed you, as well. I was only waiting for the class to end."

I stood, statue-still, as you undressed me. Then I waited and watched as you undressed, as well, removing your suit jacket, pressed shirt, kicking out of your pants. You have that colorful carpet on the floor, and we made do with that for our first bed, moving our bodies in the standard sixty-nine, my hair spread out over your thighs, your tongue probing my nether lips like a divining rod in search of my pleasure spot.

I was moaning, calling out words that were muffled against your rock-like cock, writhing sweetly as you probed me with your long fingers, with your splendid fist. You knew exactly how to work me, knew the way I longed to be treated. You made me feel passion, lust, just as you'd made me feel the words of Shakespeare for the first time. You plucked at my clit with your teeth, wrapped it around with your tongue. You rubbed your head back and forth so that your hair tickled my thighs while your fingers filled me up. I was lost in the multitude of sensations, so lost that when I heard you murmuring words into my pussy, I couldn't decipher whether you were saying my name, or speaking.

I came on the vibrations of your words, rocked by the sense that you were taking me to a higher level, a plane I'd never hit before. And then, as I slowly relaxed into those lazy, wondrous circles, I listened to the lullaby of your voice, still crooning to me, responding to my note with your own Shakespearean sonnet.

"The expense of spirit in a waste of shame is lust in action; and, till action, lust...."

Beethoven's Exiles

I love the symphony. There's something so exciting, so exhilarating, about taking part in such an age-old tradition, of being wrapped up in the soothing cocoon of 500 years of classical music. I always feel a part of something, a participant in an honored ritual.

But if I'm truly honest with myself, that's not why I love it so much. I love the symphony because we dress up for it, especially on opening night, and you look absolutely incredible in a tux.

This year we've got season tickets, the only way to get a seat at this sold-out opening. It's no wonder, since the program is so auspicious, as the classical DJs on our local station might say. A visiting world-class violinist from Moscow, the symphony's world-famous conductor, and Beethoven's glorious 9th.

There's something else that makes me like the symphony, though. While I know you love classical music, you have a tendency to get antsy around the second movement. Tonight, though, I've planned something to keep you utterly focused. Not on the music, maybe, but focused nonetheless.

It's dark in the symphony hall, so no one can see that you've slipped your hand onto my knee beneath the hem of my semi-formal dress. That's all the encouragement I need to follow through with my naughty plan. I turn and kiss you, my tongue grazing your lower lip, as I take your hand in mine and press it deeper under my dress, beneath my panties.

When your finger touches my pussy, finding it smooth, I have to fight to keep from crying out, to keep from moaning.

I watch your eyes go wide as you discover how wet I am. A moment later, my hand brushes your lap and I discover the bulge in your pants.

A few minutes after that, the hall breaks out into applause. As the performers take their standing ovation, you and I remain seated, your hand having descended back onto my knee, your middle finger now glistening with my juice.

The lights go on. "Let's go into the lobby," you tell me. "I'd love some refreshment."

I don't know why I think you mean we're going to the snack bar. It's always mobbed, and who wants an eight dollar glass of Merlot in a plastic cup, anyway? Your arm around my shoulders, you guide me toward the balcony. The symphony hall has this gorgeous balcony that overlooks the city. It's one of the most incredible views I've ever seen. Outside are the smokers, the symphony's exiles with their expensive French cigarettes, bogarting them like they were generic brands. We've been coming here for years, and there have been fewer and fewer of them each season. Now, there's nothing but a cloud of smoke and a few scattered oldsters, puffing away.

You lead me to the balcony, stand behind me, put your arms around me. Gently, you push me up against the metal railing.

"Look at the city," you say disingenuously as your hands slip under my dress. "Isn't it beautiful?"

"What are you doing?" I squeak, feeling your thumbs find the edges of my underwear. I always wear something sexy to the symphony because we always end up making love afterwards. Okay, I admit it, that's probably the real reason I love the symphony so much. I don't know if it's because these are the only occasions when we make time to go out together, or because Beethoven makes me horny. But we always make love, and so I always wear something lacy

This time it's black lace, almost see-through, and you make short work of it. I look over my shoulder, breathing heavily as you slip the elastic band over the smooth curve of my ass. My panties go sliding down my thighs and bunch around my ankles.

"Step out of them," you tell me.

I look back over my shoulder, to where the smokers are lost in their reverie, talking about whatever it is smokers talk about. I obediently step out of my underwear.

"Oh, look," you say loudly. "Somebody dropped a quarter!"

You bend down, pick up my underwear. When you stand, you casually toss it over the railing.

"Hey!" I say weakly. "You're going to pay for those, mister."

I picture some unfortunate pedestrian several stories below, hurrying to the restaurant for a nice dinner with friends and ending up, quite unexpectedly, with my panties on their head. Wet panties.

"Don't even try to tell me," you growl into my ear. "Those were soaked."

You're cuddling me from behind, your hands smooth down my belly. Your body blocks the view of the smokers, but I check several times over my shoulder just to make sure they're not watching. Then I feel your hand between my legs, and I shut my eyes tight, my heart pounding.

"Open them," you whisper, your breath warm against my ear.

I can't even think to disobey. I wouldn't want to. I don't even care if all the smokers in the symphony, all the smokers in the world, think I'm a shameless slut. I spread my legs just a little, and your hand goes under my dress, touching my pussy. It's slick with excitement, and you begin to caress my slit.

"So it's true," you say. "Beethoven makes you wet."

"What can I say? I'm partial to Romantic composers."

I gasp as your fingers slide into me.

"And Germans," I say. "And deaf guys."

"Three for three," you tell me, your lips grazing my neck. "You must be going mad with desire."

"I am," I sigh. "If Beethoven were alive, I'd track him down and fuck him." Then a shudder goes through my body as you press my clit firmly, and I press my ass back against your body. I lean heavily against the railing, careful not to stick my head over far enough to see whoever is standing down there with panties on their head, pointing up and screaming in rage.

I don't know why I do it; I just can't stop myself. I reach behind me and press my palm to your crotch, feeling how hard you've gotten in your tuxedo pants.

I turn my head to kiss you, my lips parting.

The smokers are gone.

I whisper, "We're going to miss the next movement."

I don't want to stop, and you look like you're not going to let me go. But it's Beethoven. I slip out of your grasp and take your hand, leading you back into the symphony hall. My thighs feel slick with moisture, tiny droplets of sweat soaking my dress in the small of my back. My nipples are hard, incredibly hard, showing plainly through the semi-formal dress. God, it looks so slutty to be wearing a dressy outfit like this with my nipples showing so plainly, my pussy bare and wet underneath.

The lobby is empty. Beyond, I can hear the soft strains of Beethoven's symphony beginning.

Standing at the door to the hall is a black-clad college student with glasses.

"We've closed the doors. You'll have to wait."

"But this is the last movement!" I say.

"I'm sorry."

"It's the chorus..."

"My apologies, but it's Symphony policy."

I sigh, shut my eyes. I can't believe we're going to miss the last movement because you started feeling me up. When I open my eyes and look at you, you're staring at me.

"I guess we should just leave," I say, thinking you want to take me home and fuck me.

You say: "No, we shouldn't."

You take my hand and lead me back out to the balcony. Now there's no one out there, no one at all. We've got the place to ourselves, and you lose all sense of discretion. You shove me up against the railing, kissing me hard, your tongue finding mine as your hands caress my tits through the expensive dress. My erect nipples explode with sensitivity, your thumbs sending little quivers through my body as you press against them. You reach down and pull up my dress, all the way up to my waist. The night air feels cold on my bare pussy. I grope for your belt as you kiss my neck.

I can hear the symphony faintly, launching into Schiller's chorus. Even dim and distant like that, it's beautiful.

"What if someone sees?" I ask breathlessly.

"They'll have to bring their own wife," you tell me.

Your cock comes free and I take it into my hands, moaning softly. Spreading my legs against you as you push me up against the cold metal.

"I hope this railing holds," I say.

"I'm sure it will. What do you think those season tickets pay for?"

You've got your hands on my ass, holding me up. I spread my thighs around your body and I feel your cock, hard against my thigh. As your hands are occupied, I reach down and guide your cockhead up to my pussy. It slides between my lips, finding my entrance and sliding in. It's a perfect fit, as always, and I moan as you enter me. Suspended in space by your strong arms, I feel your hips pumping in time with mine. You hit every spot, like you always do, your cock tugging my lips down to stimulate my clit, the head of it hitting that spot that makes me gasp. Every time we fuck, it feels this good. But now, my whole body is alive with the excitement and the fear of being discovered.

In the distance, I can hear the rising choral strains of 'Ode to Joy.' My cries mingle with it as you turn me around, bending me over the railing. I grip it tightly, looking down at the pedestrians walking far below, none of them knowing what we're doing up here.

You enter me from behind, reaching around to rub my clit as you fuck me. You know how to make me come, and everything about the way you're giving me your cock tells me that's what you want, more than anything.

Because I'm going to come, just at the crescendo.

I push back onto you, my ass caressed by the silky fabric of your tuxedo. Your hand on my clit drives me over the edge and I grab the railing tightly as I come. I can't stop myself from crying out, and I join the chorus with my supplication, the distant voice of Beethoven's exiles.

Then I feel it, the quickening in your thrusts that tells me it's your turn. You always let me come first; it's one of the things I love about you. But I sense you've been holding back, and now it's just a series of powerful, unforgiving thrusts before you let go inside me, your cock pulsing and filling me with your come.

When you pull out, I feel an ache, an absence, one only partially filled by the faraway coda of Ludwig's masterpiece.

I turn around and you kiss me, your arms going around me and pulling me against you.

"Did you enjoy the symphony?" you say, smiling.

"What symphony?" I ask.

A Decadent Dessert

After dinner, you tell me you've made dessert.

"Really?" I'm surprised. I didn't know you could cook.

"Really," you say, "at least, I'm *going* to make dessert. Or, rather," you say, after another healthy pause for effect, "you're going to *be* dessert."

You grin in your most seductive way, and I find myself growing incredibly aroused. Not just because I've always had something of a sweet tooth, but because you're gazing at me with a look I've never really seen on your face before. I know arousal. I know when you're sexed up. But this is different. This is much more sly.

Quickly, you strip me out of my clothes. Then you lift me and set me down on our large dining room table. I feel the slick surface of the old-fashioned cherry-printed oilcloth, and I wonder why that rubbery sensation is making me wet. With a wink, you reach for our handcuffs (stashed under your chair) and bind my wrists. Then you tell me to wait, that you'll be right back. So I wait, cuffed there, growing wetter by the second. I'm making a little puddle beneath me, but I can't help that. There's nothing I can do about being so damn excited.

When you come back, I see the blindfold in your hand. See it only for a moment, before you slide that slim piece of fabric over my eyes and then tie it into place beneath my hair. As soon as the blindfold is in place, I feel a transformation. I don't know if the lights are still on or if you've turned them off. I don't know if you're close to me, or if you're across the room watching. I feel warning lights going off in my head, and I shift on the tablecloth, waiting impatiently for whatever you have planned. I hear you leave the room again, and I wonder how long you'll make me wait for you. Will you make me beg? Will you hear me if I do?

In only a moment, you come back, and I hear the shift and settling of contents on the table next to the bed. But I have no idea what toys or tools you've brought with you.

"Patience," you say. "Relax and let me take care of you."

The very first sensation is cold. Ice cold. In fact, ice cream. I cry out as you run a spoon filled with steadily melting ice cream along the hollow of my throat, then trace it over the rise of my breasts. I feel the sweet liquid trickling along the cracks and crevasses, but I am now much more aware of the other trickling sensation. For some reason, being plunged into this world of not-knowing has made my pussy dripping.

You use the ice cream until it has completely melted, and now I feel something else, something sticky and thick—molasses? Chocolate syrup? I draw in a breath to see if I can tell, and now I know, immediately—butterscotch. Your very favorite of the topping flavors. You go to work with your tongue, cleaning me immediately. And I feel a new sticky sensation as my pussy continues to churn forth the steady supply of nectar. But when are you going there? Not yet. You're too busy with....

Don't know what this is at all. You apply it with your fingertips. Not a liquid. A cream... Not whipped cream. Icing. I realize that now, icing. You frost my pussy completely, and I think I'm going to lose it as your fingers fully coat my inner lips, pinching slightly as you hold them apart. And then finally, you're dining on me. Just me. I can imagine the way your face looks coated with my juices and the store-bought whipped frosting, but I can't see you. I can only feel you licking at me, lapping like a cat to finish off a saucer of milk. Or a saucer, in this case, of cream. Sweet drippy cream.

When you pull away, I moan, but you're not finished, you're just ready for a little sixty-nine action. I am surprised at the first taste before I realize you've coated yourself in the vanilla frosting, as well, and now, I simply part my lips and take you down, swallowing against your rod, unable to help myself. I lick the icing off your cock as if I'm the hungriest person who's ever lived. And then I just lick your cock. Lick and lap and swallow it down, knowing that we are both coated and sticky in all the confectionery toppings—a decadent dessert, created just for two.

Deja Nude

We've been here before. That's the first thought that slips through my head as I watch you undress. The heat beating between us is an echo of heat from another time. Long ago. So faint and faraway that I can't place it. Yet the things you say, every whisper, ever sex-drenched word, are reverberations of the come-ons you've uttered before. There's comfort to me in reliving a uniquely spectacular time. And I would relax into the feeling of enjoying a second-go-round. Except that although the feeling of recreating a specific event is alive and vibrating in my mind, it can't possibly be true. This is the first time for us. So no matter what my mind is telling me, I know it's only a serious case of deja vu.

Or in this case, *deja nude*.

I watch in happy silence as you peel off your suit jacket and hang it on the back of my wooden chair. Then I watch, just as pleased, as you slowly undo the row of buttons on your pressed white shirt. You're taking your time, which I appreciate. This is the first evening that we've been naked together, and even though I think we've done it before, I want to savor every moment of your slow and steady strip-tease.

You can't do it without a smile, though. We're not the sort of people who can pull something like this off with a straight face. So as you kick off your shoes and lose your pants, you even hum a little bit of 'The Stripper' under your breath. And even that is a reminder to me of some imaginary time. I know each part of this evening. I know what it will feel like when you reach for me on the bed and grab me. I'll giggle as you trace your fingers along the lines of my body.

I'll squirm and try to pull away, but you won't let me, because you'll know that I don't want to get away. I want to get even closer to you.

Now that you're naked, it's my turn. I stand in the center of the bed and peel my skimpy pink dress over my head. Then I bounce in place, shaking the mattress, and you reach and make me tumble. We fall into the pillows, laughing, and then you start to tickle me, just as I knew you would.

Your fingers are relentless, and I find my body thrusting upwards to meet them. I want your roaming hands everywhere: along my ribs, under my chin. Tickling and caressing until I'm too worked up to think or speak, too shaken by laughter to make any coherent statements.

Truthfully, I don't need to say anything. The outrageously heady scent of my arousal is rich in the air around us, and as you keep tickling me with your knowing fingertips, your lips take part in the action, moving lower along my body until you find the junction between my thighs. Breathless with laughter, I still know what to do. That deja vu thing kicking in again, let's me know that at this moment I should swivel my body around until we are in a sixty-nine. I open my lips around the head of your cock and take you in. The taste of you is immediately relaxing to me. Your skin is dreamy sweet and manly. I can't get enough of your cock in my throat. As you work me between my legs, I work you back, mirroring and echoing, keeping up with you and slowing down.

But you aren't ready for finish lines yet. Swiftly, you pull away from me, and now I see that you have planned for this evening very carefully. On the bedside table is a lone feather. Long and white, so intricate, so delicate.

"Hold still," you say, and I lock my eyes on yours as you run the feather down one of my arms and up the other. I'm trembling and shivering at the tickling sensation.

"Come on," you urge, "don't make me tie you."

It's something someone would say to a long-time partner, isn't it? Some casual comment thrown out there. Heed my wishes, or I will capture you to the bed. I can see that in my head, a vision which is the opposite of deja vu. A future fantasy, which unfolds immediately in my mind.

I don't have any time to think about that, though, because now you are working me more seriously, running the tip of the feather along my belly, then over my breasts and in circles around my nipples. I can feel how wet I'm getting. I know you know. You have to know. But you don't stop. You run the feather between my thighs, up one and down the other, teasing but not touching my pussy.

Now, I'm gasping for air between giggles, and I'm almost helpless to do anything. Anything, that is, except suck you again. Because before I can ask for mercy, you're on me in a sixty-nine once more, and I am drinking from you as I've never sucked any man's cock. My body is alive with fierce shuddering. I'm still on edge, on fire, from the tickling, but now I have a much more pressing desire. I want to drain you. I want to swallow every drop.

We are so busy pleasing each other that each one of us loses the concept of our own pleasure. I don't even realize that I'm about to come until I do. Grinding my hips against your mouth I find instant blissful release and it shakes me until I realize that you're coming with me, shooting down my throat, filling me up.

We are connected so tightly that it takes a moment for us to pull back and untangle ourselves. And even as we're moving, I realize that we're only rearranging our bodies for the next situation. This time, I'll be on the top, and you'll take your place again right where I want you.

But this time, the deja vu will be for real.

Ancient History

My first memory of you is popcorn-scented. Popcorn-scented and *Mad Max*-infused. I know that wouldn't make much sense to most people. Doesn't sound like a romantic Hallmarkcard sentiment. Or "scentiment," really. But it is.

There you were—three rows ahead of me and my friend Janet. We sat at the Varsity Theater on New Year's Day from 8 p.m. until some wee hour in the morning watching all three of the *Mad Max* movies in a row. Thinking back, I realize that it was a crazy thing to do to kick off the New Year. We didn't care. The trilogy was just something to kill the time on a day filled with hangovers and freshly broken resolutions. But after catching sight of you, I didn't see much of the on-screen action.

I don't know how you and I made the connection in the dark balcony of that dilapidated theater—but we did. I knew you'd seen me, because you kept turning around to check me out. I learned the look of your face in that odd blue glow of the flickering celluloid. At the first intermission, you asked my name. At the second, you held my hand for a moment, squeezing my fingertips as you got me to tell you about myself. After the final movie, when it was too late to call it late anymore, and too early to call it dawn, we went out behind the theater to the graffiti-decorated alley, and you pressed me up against the wall and kissed me.

I know every part of that kiss—your warm hands cradling my face, your fingers in my hair. The harsh-sweet roughness of your morning shadow. The dangerous softness of your lips. Beyond that, I know the excitement of your body, that hard necessary presence against me when you bit into my bottom lip. And I know that you didn't fuck me that night, even though I would have let you. Even though I would have begged you to if I'd had the guts. Would have told you to lower my jeans and do me in the alley. Do me until I screamed. I could already taste how good it would be. The thrilling way your body would press against mine. The wetness of my sex as I enveloped you.

Instead, you handed me a piece of paper that had your name and number scribbled on it, and you motioned for me to go to where my friend was waiting in the parking lot, already half-asleep in her convertible Rabbit, rock 'n roll music on loud.

"See you," you said, as I walked away.

My second memory of you is the heart-pounding, blood-rushing in my ears feeling of holding your note in my hand and reading the words: *This may sound crazy, but call me tomorrow. I need to know you.*

Tomorrow was actually today—but I waited until noon before dialing your digits, and when I heard your voice on the other end of the line, my breath caught and I forgot what my name was or how to speak. Luckily, you understood, and you set a time and promised to meet me at my work, said you'd walk me home.

We didn't make it home. No big surprise there. My legs were weak and watery simply from the touch of your hand in mine. We made it to a park bench half a mile from my house, and you kissed me again, kissed me hard, and I felt myself falling. I've never had a kiss like that since then, although I've judged all other kisses by that one. Hand in hand, we walked back downtown to the alley behind the Varsity, and this time, when you kissed me, I felt you lift me in your arms, felt you press me against those painted words and pictures. I had my hand on your button fly, pulling on it, but you shook your head. That wasn't the way you wanted us to start.

Back at your place, you showed me what it meant—what everyone was talking about—what the whole big deal was. You spread me out on your mattress and you kissed me everywhere—my fingertips, my breasts, the soft indents at the backs of my knees. You kissed the nape of my neck and along my ribs, and when I started to sigh, you parted my legs and kissed me there.

I was glad I'd waited, that I hadn't given in to some boy in the back seat of his daddy's car. Was thrilled that you were able to teach exactly what I so desperately wanted to learn. How to give in. How to lie back and take it. I covered my face with my hands because it felt so good, and I was embarrassed at how I must look. Untamed and out of control. Those descriptions had never suited me before.

"Stop—" you told me. "Don't hide. Let me see you—"

And you pulled my hands away and went back to your tickling, kissing games. You spiraled your tongue over my clit, and then licked gently in slow, sensuous circles on the insides of my thighs. I thought I would cry. The pleasure from your warm, knowing mouth was so intense. I thought I would scream, but I didn't know how. I've never been one to let loose like that. I've always been caught up in a mess of thoughts—how will I look? What will he think?

"Relax," you said. "Don't worry. Just relax."

And I let myself. Let myself get there with you. With the help of your mouth and your fingers, and finally the rock-solid hardness of your cock as you thrust it inside me. You looked down at me as you pushed up and slid back in. You held my gaze with your gleaming eyes and you whispered sweet nonsense words to me. Until I was coming. With you. Through you. Coming so hard.

*****

We spent most of that final semester in your bed. I ducked out of class early, took a cab to your place, lied to cover my tracks. I had a difficult time lying to my friends, to my family. I've always been the good girl, never caused anyone a moment's trouble.

Didn't have to. With you, I didn't cause any trouble either. I melted into your sheets, against your skin, mouth open to drink in your cock. Anything you said, I did. When you told me to take my panties down, slip them off, and go bare, I obeyed. I went out to dinner with you with no panties on under my short skirt. I let you press me up in the unisex bathroom of the restaurant and fuck me while a line formed outside of patrons waiting impatiently to get in.

You taught me everything I know. You taught me how to give pleasure—with my mouth and my body and my voice. And you taught me how to take pleasure, how not to hide from the desires that burned within me. Because they've been there all along. Those needs. Those requests. Silent and smothered, they waited for someone like you to come along.

And you did—like the prince in the fairy tale. You came along.

But the thing of it was, you couldn't stay.

My last memory of you is from six months later. I hate to think of goodbyes, of what would have happened if I'd been a different kind of person, of why it all came apart. But even though we're not together, and even though I don't know where you are, or whatever happened to you, I judge all others by you, and none has ever come close to erasing that popcorn-scented dream that you created.

Untouched

When you start out in this world, you think you actually invented something. You're naive, right? You have the nerve to think that *you* actually invented something new. This is before you really get involved, before you learn about the true underground world that exists below us. The parallel world, spinning backwards on the same axis. The fringe.

Then suddenly, you get a peek behind closed doors, and you realize that there isn't anything new to invent. There isn't one single thing that someone, somewhere, hasn't already done before you. And probably a hell of a lot better than you, novice that you are.

Of course, I'm not saying that within the boundaries, things can't be changed. Without a doubt, you bring something unique to the scene. You'll bring your own *je ne se quois*, your own signature scent, but all that you own that is truly you, that is *truly* original, is your DNA. And you didn't even invent that. You've got to give your parents, your grandparents, and your ancestors credit for that.

Still, I'm hard-headed. It took me so long to learn those simple facts. It took hitting walls and trying to knock them down all by myself. Ultimately, it took meeting you.

When I was younger, I used to try to find one place that no one else had ever stepped on—one piece of Earth to claim as my own. Walking along the beach, I'd think, "No one has ever been exactly here, before." But then I'd see a footprint, or, many footprints, so I'd change the phrasing to suit my needs: "No one has ever been exactly here, wearing exactly this bathing suit; no one with black curly hair, chocolate brown eyes, and a birthmark shaped like Italy has ever stood right here, right now." (A bit too far too go to be original.)

I'm laughing to myself, because even though I've gotten over this, I can remember that desperate feeling, the craving for being unique. For some of us have that need, to find it, to own it, to discover virginal, unclaimed land. And that's what I thought I did, the first time I let you fasten a studded collar around my throat and attach a rippling, silver chain.

New to me, that's honest enough. So new. The frighteningly sexy sensation of being harnessed for your will. Or, more honest, still, for your pleasure.

But how could I have kidded myself into thinking that you and I were sexual pioneers? I'm not dumb. I knew you had to be buying our toys somewhere, that there was actually a factory churning out this stuff. Still, I managed to convince myself that the things we did, the games we played, were *ours* alone. Dressing up naughty, like your little baby-girl. Calling you Daddy, acting the role of a bad school girl, your slut. Wearing skins, playing at being tough.

What a fucking joke.

When I eventually arrived on the scene, I learned that not only did I *not* invent this shit—everyone else seemed to already know about it. Everyone. It felt like being left out of a secret. Or not invited to a birthday party in elementary school. I felt like a loser.

Worse than that.

I felt lost.

Ah, but I was one of the lucky few. 'Cause you found me... and claimed me ... and made me your own. Untouched, I was, a journal waiting to be filled, an empty glass waiting for a shot of whiskey, a naked wrist waiting for the pull of a tight, metal cuff. Untouched, I was, and pure. And you found me and made me all dirty.

"You're mine," you said, "You are mine." First words, whispered to me in the back room of Old Joe's, whispered right up against my ear, because the rhythm section of the band was shaking the walls and the crowd around us were laughing loudly at some funny story the bartender had told.

I lowered my mascara-drenched lashes and inclined my head slightly toward you. I'd heard the words you said, but I wanted to be sure. You got the gesture immediately, and you slid your strong, dark arm around my waist and pulled me in closer. We couldn't have gotten any closer than that—blood and bones and thin, fine skin were the only things separating our beating hearts, and our hard/wet bodies.

"You're mine." Your arm pulled me so firmly, and I could feel the links of your silvery wallet chain digging into my thigh. "Come on, girl, time to go."

Discovered. (*No.* No. Rediscovered.)

I went, willingly (I must say that, now, willingly), followed you through the throng of multi-colored, multi-sexed dancers, down the dark hallway, and out the back door. The cool air slapped me, stunning me, and I realized I'd left my coat under the bar stool. No worries, your strong arms were around me again, warming me, leading me to your shiny red pickup.

"Seen you around, baby, but never alone."

"We split," I said, motioning to the place on my hand where a ring used to be but now wasn't. (But it had been, understand that, there was no territory on my body that had not been previously claimed by someone else, was there?)

"What'cha doing here, then, darling? This was his hang-out, wasn't it?"

Shake of my head, of my long, black hair, letting it tickle against my cheeks and the naked part of my back that my dress didn't cover. "No, sir. This was mine." Claim it, you get it? Make it your own.

"Okay, all right. But what'cha doin' here, tonight, darling? Who you looking for?"

A step closer, a step further away from my past and toward the thrilling danger of my future—into the tight, choking hold of my present. "You." A laugh, one that didn't sound at all like my own. A laugh and an up-from-under look that was meant to be bashful, that was meant to show my faith in your power. "I was waiting for you."

No words, then, just that tight grip around my wrist, leading me to your truck. The music of your key sliding into the lock, the click of the door as it swung open, ready to swallow me up. Your hand on my ass, lifting me into the seat. Then silence, as the world slowed while you stalked around the truck and then got in on the driver's side.

"Waiting for me," you said under your breath as the ignition caught and we exited the parking lot. "What do you know about me?"

Head lowered, staring at the crotch of my dress, wanting to see if the wetness had spread through panties, nylons, slip, and stretchy black jersey. "I know." A beat. "I know what you can do."

Claim me. Own me. Find something new.

Your turn to laugh, now, your turn to find a joke where there was none.

"You know, huh? How do you know?"

We made a left off the main drag, into the windy streets of the bordering residential neighborhood. Not a nice neighborhood, but home to many of the patrons who hang at Old Joe's. Apartments with crumbling red brick facades, tiny forgotten bungalows that don't take up enough space to be a threat to anyone. Yards of clotheslines connecting the buildings and colorful tatters of T-shirts and jeans pinned onto the lines, blowing in the breeze like broken and forgotten kites caught in trees.

"How'd you know?" Your voice was darker with the repetition, and I realized, quickly, that when you asked a question, you meant it to be answered.

"Trinket," I mumbled, calling the bartender, Katarina, by her nickname, "Trinket told me about you and her, about what you did together. About what *you* did to her."

"She show you, as well?"

"Yes," a pause, "Sir."

"She show you everything?"

A nod, trembling one, and then again, "Yes, Sir."

"And you still wanted to be with me?"

"No, Sir. I wanted to be ... yours."

"Ah," you said, a smile in your voice, I could hear it, though I didn't dare look up. "But, darling, that's what it means. When you're with me, you are mine. That's the point, darling. That's the whole fuckin' point."

The tattoo on Trinket's back had told me as much, the drifting colors, shifting patterns. The lock in the center with the word "slave" all but carved out in bold relief. And to be yours was more than an honor—it was a lifelong commitment.

We'd reached your studio, the converted garage behind your tiny house. I'd heard of it, of course, but never been there. It's by invitation only, you understand. It's a private party, and if you don't know the password, you don't get in. I waited for you to kill the engine, waited while you climbed out of the car and walked to my side to open my door. That's the way you are. I'd heard that before. You play with etiquette the way some people twirl their hair around one finger, or bite their bottom lip with nervousness. You play with manners like a nervous twitch, holding doors open for your ladies, pulling out their chairs, paying, always paying (with cash, that is—the women you date pay with something much more dear).

Your hand slid up from my wrist to my forearm, and you closed your fist tightly, as if testing my muscles, as if wondering whether I'd have the strength to fight. I wouldn't fight. I wanted to tell you. Because each time you touched me it happened—I felt new. I felt molded, as your hands moved up and down my arms, squeezing, releasing.

Create me, I wanted to beg. *Make me into something new. Something yours.*

The Vasco de Gama of love...

I wondered if we'd go to the house, first, or start off in the studio. I knew what I wanted, but I wasn't going to say a word until you asked me a question. The rules, again, the regulations. So important for a good scene. Deathly important for a starting relationship. Like a dance, a two-step, you have to work together. And if someone trips, if someone stumbles, there is a type of embarrassment that can destroy a budding love affair. Any good dancer will tell you that: you need to watch your partner, you need to learn from the way you are touched, from the look in your partner's eyes, from the very rhythm of their breathing.

You never watch their feet—that's not where the magic is. You watch their eyes, or you close your eyes, and you watch their soul.

And with you, there was something else, something beyond that simple, petty, one two three, one two three. There was something darker in those cavernous eyes, in the strength of your fingers, in the wisdom of your expression as you stared at me.

"Trinket showed you. But you still don't get it, do you?"

I bit my lip to keep from saying something stupid. You were right. I didn't get it—I was functioning on a need, not on smarts at this point.

"Ask me questions, now," you said. "I want to know what you want to know. I want to know what you're thinking."

"How many?" I mumbled, aware of how carefully you arranged the situation—you standing, me sitting, you free in the outdoors, me trapped in the metal cage of the truck. Everything with a meaning—everything with a new meaning.

"How many... women?" I said, finishing the questioning, knowing that you wouldn't think to guess what I had meant. That you would wait for me to be specific.

"Does it matter?"

I thought about it. "No." It didn't matter at all—I'd wondered, curiously, how many of the women at Old Joe's, at Sindy's, at Marlena's Watering Hole were yours. But it didn't affect me, either way.

"Next question." Your hand on me knee gave me the strength to continue.

"How long will it take?"

"Forever."

"To do the artwork, I mean."

"Forever."

I shook my head. "I don't understand."

"I've been waiting for you. You can understand that, can't you? I've been waiting for you as you've been waiting for me. You will be my art in progress. You will be my only one. The others—for me—were practice. That was the same way with you and him, wasn't it?"

I nodded. I hadn't even allowed myself to hope for something like this. I only wanted... what did I want? I only wanted to feel it, to feel the light that shined in Trinket's eyes. To feel the world stop beneath me, the fringe world, the parallel world, as I yawned and stretched and came, once more, to life.

"Yes, sir," I said softly, "Yes, sir, I understand."

"Do you want this?"

Emphatically, "Oh, yes. More than anything."

"Good." Your hand on my knee slid upward to my thigh, then my crotch, cupping me there, adding a pressure that I was not used to. "You will be mine," you said. "This is mine."

I nodded. "Yes, Sir."

"Come with me."

Slid out of the truck bed, slammed the door, and followed you to the garage, watched you undo the padlock and chain, slide the wood door open and step outside to wait for me. I walked in ahead of you, into darkness, not able to make out anything in the room. There was a click as you flicked on the lights and the room glowed in modern beauty.

You had a tattoo parlor in your garage. The chair, the designs on the walls, the needles, the ink. You had everything, sterile, perfectly in place. Beaming skulls grinned down at me. Roses curled with daggers. Tigers pranced back and forth. Skeletons shimmered in stark black line. All done by your hand. All done by a master.

"You don't get to choose," you said, talking casually as you began to set up the needles and inks.

"I know."

"But you can let me know what you like."

I wandered around, looking at the walls, trying to decide which scrolling piece I liked the best. Because they'd all been created by you, I could not choose one over the other. Each had a stark beauty, a inner glow, unlike any of the work I'd seen by artists in other tattoo parlors.

"You don't like anything?"

"I like everything."

Now you put down your instruments and came over to me, catching my face between your hands and kissing me. "You know that I do this for a living, right?"

"Yes."

"You know that in the future I will tattoo other people?"

"Yes."

"But from now on I tattoo you only with my own designs. You don't choose from the walls. You don't pick tigers and ladies behind partially opened doors. No ravens in windows. No pin-up Bettys. I create art for your body, for your skin, and you close your eyes and feel the pain of the needle as it reaches beneath your skin, as it reaches to your soul."

"Yes."

"You will be mine." You looked at me with your dark eyes in your dark face, "No, no, you're already mine."

You led me to the chair and after a moment's thought, fastened me down with leather straps. Then, slowly, you slid a pair of steel scissors underneath the hem of my dress and slip and cut all the way to the neckline. The cold metal against my skin made me tremble, but I remained as still as I could as you parted the two halves of the dress and revealed my pale skin.

Your fingers tested each part of my exposed body, the way an artist checks a canvas to make sure it is evenly stretched over a frame. You stroked my throat, my breasts, the sides of my ribs. You placed the palms of both hands against my belly, feeling the spot where my pulse still raced. You cupped your hand again over my mound of pubis (through my panties) and smiled as you felt the wetness seep through the crotch and to your fingers.

"We'll start tonight," you said. "I will not tell you what I am drawing. I will not be working from a set design, only from the pictures I see in my mind."

"Yesss..."

Claim me. Own me. Find something new.

Quickly, you prepared the needle, choosing the first color, dark blood red, and moving in close. And, with your assistance, I did invent something new. With your help, I reinvented *myself*.

Blind Date

You said the guy was perfect for me. Exactly what I was looking for.

"How do *you* know what I'm looking for?" I asked.

"Trust me," you said, winking. "I know." You smiled, then, and added, "Sometimes blind dates are the best kinds. The thrill of anticipation, right? Potential magic waiting to happen."

I took a deep breath, considering it. I hadn't been on a date in awhile. Not a real date, anyway. I'd been slumming, hitting the bar scene maybe too heavily, winding up in strange beds and slinking home before the owners of those beds awoke and started doing a post-mortem on the previous evening's activities.

"One night," you promised, running your fingers through your dark hair to push it out of your eyes "What's one night out of your whole life?"

"Fine," I said, more to quiet you than anything else. When you get hold of an idea, you don't let up easily. But that Saturday night, as I got ready, I actually found myself excited. Nervous, butterfly-excited. I spent an extra-long time with my makeup, outlining my eyes with the new gold liquid liner I'd bought on a whim. It made my brown eyes look Cleopatra-like, which I thought was rather sexy. I brushed my thick, black hair until it gleamed with a tempered blue halo.

Standing in my black, lace lingerie, I agonized over my outfits before choosing a berry-red dress, one I'd never worn but had mocked me from the back of my closet for too long.

With it, I wore the matching red heels I'd bought.

The doorbell rang while I was dabbing perfume at my pulse points, a scent called Curve that I'd bought for the bottle. I smiled at my reflection in the hallway mirror before opening the door, to reveal my blind date.

When I saw you, I have to admit, I did not immediately get it. "What's up?"

"Ready?" you asked, moving past me into the living room, your arms filled with flowers, your body sleek and lean in leather pants and a leather vest. I followed and stood as you made yourself comfortable on my sofa. You'd sat there often in the past, but somehow you looked like a stranger to me this time.

"Who'd you expect?" you asked, making me feel like a complete and total idiot.

"Oh..." I stammered. "You, of course, *you*. I knew it was you all along." Maybe because I continued to prattle, you stood and grabbed me around the waist, silencing me with your lips on mine. Regardless of the reason for your actions, the kiss did the trick, hushing me, making my body come alive in your arms while clamming up my vocal cords.

You moved away and said, "You know I'm right for you. Think about it while I take your dress off." I stood absolutely still as you unzipped me, undid my bra, unhooked my garters. I thought of all the fun we have together, the way we can finish each other's sentences like an old married couple. Then I stopped thinking as you bent me over my sofa and undid your leather slacks, letting me feel the skin of your outfit against my naked skin before diving inside me with your oh-so-ready cock.

I gripped onto the sofa pillows to steady myself, but you would have none of it, obviously trying to keep me continually off-guard. You grabbed my wrists and pulled them behind my back, anchoring both in one of your large hands. I didn't struggle too hard, not even when I felt the cuffs slip over them and clink shut. You'd come prepared.

"Take it," you said. "You deserve this... for all the times you've spent telling me about your whorish ways. For all the times you made me listen, rather than letting me do what we both know should have been done a long, long time ago." Captured like that, I didn't have much of a choice. But I didn't want much of a choice. I felt you slam into me, felt it in the depth of my being, and I relished it. Each stroke was perfection.

"You don't have to slink home anymore," you said.

I shuddered, unable to answer.

"You just have to face me, every morning, in our bed."

You knew exactly how I wanted to be touched, the hard palm of your hand coming down and connecting, firmly, with my ass. Repeatedly, accentuating the way you were fucking me.

You're right about a lot of things. It's why you've always been my prize confidant. You were right about us, too. How well we fit together, our bodies, our desires. You rode me, pressing me against the sofa, making it hurt while you made me come. Sublime. After, basking in that warm, golden glow, you repeated your words of wisdom, "Sometimes blind dates are the best kind."

And, knowing you were right this time, I just smiled.

You Wear It Well

Some men would look silly in this outfit—but not you. I mean, fuck, you look hot and ready and ripe. When you emerge from the bedroom in the matte black corset that I bought for you, the garterless fishnets, spikey high heels, all I can think is how much I want to fuck you. But I make myself back off, try to force myself to go slow.

Mentally, I picture each frame. I see myself pressing my body to yours. Feeling the glossy softness of the expensive material against my skin. Feeling your skin between the laces, above the garters, under the silk. I want to drive my fingers beneath the boundaries of the fabric and touch you. Just touch you. Then I want to bend you over, show you that I'm packing a toy on my harness, and let you know what it's really like to be taken.

You're ready, aren't you? You're ready to take it.

With one hand, you cautiously motion for me to come forward, and I follow you into the bedroom and sit on the edge of the mattress, trying to drink you in. But I'm having a difficult time. I don't know where to look first.

Your hair is that birch-blonde that looks white in direct sunlight and pale like a cloud in our dimly lit room. And with your tanned skin, blue eyes, sweet pout of a mouth, I just want to eat you up.

"This is really strange—" you say, indicating your reflection in the full-length mirror that hangs on the back of the closest door. And sure, maybe it is. Maybe you've never seen yourself look pretty before, and you don't know how to deal with the image. But tonight we're playing out my fantasy—and you've agreed to let me dress you up any way I want to. You're not doing this out of the kindness of your heart—you know that when it's your turn, I'll return the favor. When you're in charge, you can put me into the clothing of your dark dreams. Dress me like a princess in a sheer white gown and petticoat. Make me up like a street whore in cheap vinyl and thigh-high boots. Put me in pasties and let me dance for you to some rocking song straight out of your high school years. Something from Zeppelin or Pink Floyd.

But right now, it's my turn. And as I come forward, standing behind you, touching you, I can tell that you don't mind. How can I tell? Because I see the bulge of your cock under those tight black satin panties. Cock and panties. Wouldn't have thought those two concepts would go together. But they do. Oh, do they ever. Your cock clad in those sweet panties is one of the sexiest sights I've ever seen. The rod of it is straining against the soft fabric, demanding attention.

Now, I know exactly what I want to do—what I have to do—and I'm fairly certain that you're not going to stop me. I don't even bother to ask. Instead, while you watch, I go down on my knees on the floor, and I run my hands up and up your fishnet-clad legs. The patterned stockings feel delightful under my palms. I've been on the inside of fishnets, but never on the outside, and now I can understand what a turn-on they are. I can see your legs, and touch your skin, but there is that deviant barrier between us. I continue to stroke you until my hands press against the crotch of those panties.

If you were a girl, your panties would be dreamy wet in the center. The cream of your arousal would be thick enough for me to taste. As it is, the rock-hard pole of your cock makes a dangerous outline beneath the fabric.

Christ, you're hard.

I press my lips against your cock through the silk, and then I use my tongue to stroke you up and down.

"That's right," you moan, and you sound exactly like the same person I know. The same person I live with and sleep with and curl up in bed with. The same man I bend over for, or ride astride, or suck off. But when I look at you, see you in this disguise, you've turned into someone else. My girl. My boy-girl. My toy.

I want to swallow you down, and I also want to press you down flat onto the bed and fuck you. Flat-out. Plain and simple. Fuck you. No image has ever been so clear in my mind before. Even though we've never played like this, somehow, I know exactly how it will feel. I'll be in charge, and you'll come because of my power. But although I'd like nothing else than to go racing toward the finish line, I force myself to start slowly, to stretch this evening out. This is a present for me. *You* are a present for me. All wrapped up in the glittering wrapping of my choosing. So now I need to take my time. I carefully lick your cock through the panties, getting the fabric wet where you can't get it wet. You sigh hard, and that urges me onward. I make my lips open and sloppy and draw as much of your satin-clad cock as I can into my mouth. You arch to help me, pushing your hips forward in a greedy way, demanding with your body that I give you more of the contact that you so desperately crave.

But I always like the feeling of being hidden at the beginning. When it's me on the receiving end of a little tongue-pleasure, I love the moments before you reveal me. When you eat me through my panties, pressing your mouth against the satin or lace or silk, I think I'll go crazy if I can't feel your tongue on my naked flesh. Now, I treat you to this same sensation, until I sense you are about to scream.

Only then do I reach up and grab hold of the waistband and slide those panties down. As I do, I think about what it feels like when you take my panties down. When you move over me on the bed and glide my underpants off and down my thighs. I tremble with the knowledge of what is about to happen. You're the one trembling now. I am extremely aware of the fact that I have a harness on under my jeans and that my cock is packed in there, getting warm from the heat of my body. It's as if that sexy toy is actually growing larger. I know this is all in my head, but I feel myself expand, as if the synthetic cock really is a part of myself.

Gingerly, you step out of the pretty panties, and then you stand there, your cock throbbing away from your body, and you wait. Aren't you behaving well for me? I know that you want to toss me onto the mattress and fuck me hard. But this is my night, my call. The wanting urges are deep in your eyes, yet to make me happy you wait. Good boy, I think as I lead you to the mattress. Sweet boy, I think as I help you to lie face down on the bed. I make my way down your body, licking from the nape of your neck to the back of your corset, touching you wherever the skin is present. I keep on licking when I reach the rise of your asscheeks, and then I part you and lick between.

You sigh again at that sexy intrusion, and I work you a little bit harder, pleased when you buck your hips against the mattress. I know what I look like in this position. We've videotaped ourselves fucking, so I know precisely how I move, how my body has a will of its own. Like yours has a will, the will to arch up and spread open and let me in deep.

When I can't wait any longer, I mean, I just can't fucking wait, I part my slacks and reveal my cock. You can't see it, but I know you hear the sound of me pouring the lube into the palm of my hand and then jacking it up and down over my cock. I love my cock. Isn't that the strangest thing ever. I love manhandling it, imagining that if I worked it just right, it would shoot across your naked ass. 'Course that's an impossibility—but you're going to shoot tonight, definitely, and it will be because of this fabulous toy.

Slowly, I set the head of it against your asshole, and I hear you drag in your breath, as if you're going to say, "No." Or "Stop." Or "Don't." But you say nothing. You just stay still and breathe, waiting for me to continue. So I do. I jog the head of my cock inside you, then rock back on my heels to pull it out. You moan then, and that lets me know that I'm doing this right. Back in I go, a little deeper this time, and you turn your head away from me and let out the tiniest whimper. And fuck, it does something inside me. That noise, almost helpless in its urgency, makes me grip into your hips and really drive hard. I am a machine now. I work you back and forth, and I find that my hands are behaving without commands from my head. My open palm connects with your bare asscheek, leaving a stinging plum-colored blow. I decorate the other side with a similar mark.

I like the sound that the spanks make, and I like the sounds that you make, and I keep on working you until I sense you're about to come. Do I stop? Do I roll you over and climb aboard? No. That's not how it should go. Instead, I keep right on fucking you, until you cream against the mattress. Only then do I whip off the harness, roll you over on the bed, and slide my pussy in front of your lips. You're still hungry, and worked up, and you let loose your pent-up emotions by licking my clit. Quick, roundy motions with the point of your tongue have me on the verge in seconds. I buck against you, just as you fucked the mattress, and I put my palms flat on the wall in front of me to hold myself steady.

When I cream, you keep licking, knowing that if you tease me onwards with just the right touch, I'll come again. But this time, I push down your body, wrap one hand around your cock, and work you until you're hard again. I want to be fucked this time. I want you to fuck me.

You can't do it while you're wearing the girly corset. You rip your way out of it, and only then do you take charge, fucking me so hard that I scream. I don't know what it is about tonight that's made us into these two wild creatures, and I don't have the time to ponder it. I simply revel in the fact that we're let loose, out of control as we come together, and then collapse in a tangled heap.

Naked on the bed, you look up at me with a glazed happy expression. The well-satisfied expression of a perfectly-fucked lover. It's an echo of the look on my own face, I'm sure. And no doubt about it, baby, you wear it well.

Blowing Smoke

I know it's sort of stupid, sort of too chic, too in the moment, but I have a thing for guys who smoke cigars. At first, I thought they were trying to be macho. Some of 'em are, I guess. Then, one night, at the Regular Cat, I saw you lighting up. Your mouth around that cigar did something to me. It made my heart beat a little too fast. I walked over and asked for another beer, and as you poured it, I breathed in, catching that odd mix of your cologne mingling with cigar smoke.

I said, "Could I try that? You look like your enjoying it."

You said, "Sure," pulled it from your mouth and passed it over. The butt of it was wet with your spit. I didn't care, though, wanted to swap spit with you in other ways. I placed the stogie in my mouth and took a puff. It was bitter, a much different experience from my regular Kools, but I didn't hate it. Though, have to admit, I liked it better when you had your lips around it.

Maybe the cigar smoke had gone to my head, because I felt more cocky than I normally am, more confident. I passed the cigar back to you and tilted my head to the side, taking you in. Your short, black hair looks like animal fur. Your eyes go back and forth between brown or black, and your skin is the dark, warm color of a chestnut.

"Wanna try something else?" you asked, and I grinned.

"When do you get off?" My voice was low, not humble, but close. You're awe-inspiring. Your tough-edged charm is exactly what makes me tick.

"When do I get off?" you repeated, slowly, mouthing the

words back at me. You looked at Kelly, your partner behind the bar, then back at me. "Well, chicklet, I guess I get off right about now."

That made sense because you're not just one of the bartenders. You're the owner of this place, which is why you didn't seem to care much about breaking the no-smoking law, or about ducking out on your shift.

You sidled out from behind the bar and grabbed my hand, leading me to the private office hidden by a wood-paneled door. Once the door was shut, I was in your arms, moving against you as if dancing, though there was no music playing. The voices of the other, not-so-lucky patrons could be heard, but I couldn't make out any words. Maybe you were dancing to that, the rise and fall of other people talking. You moved your body against mine, pressing hard with your chest and your hips and your thighs, letting me feel the raw muscles beneath the tight confines of your faded jeans. Letting me feel that you were hard, that there was just hard, taut skin under those denim threads.

I undid your vest, revealing the silken smoothness of your skin. I bent to your nipples, kissing them, lingering on them before licking in a long, smooth line down your belly to your jeans. You helped me strip off those faded 501s, then seated yourself on your desk with your thighs parted. I got on my knees in front of you and serviced you with my mouth.

You were already so fucking hard, but I made you even more so, loving your rig with my tongue and lips, teasing your cock until it was desperate to play. I followed my instincts, and knew I was on the right track when you moaned and sprawled back on the desk, kicking your legs even further apart, granting me access to the puckered opening of your asshole.

I didn't know where to go first. But finally I used my moistened finger to tickle your rosebud while I continued to pleasure you with my tongue. As I did, you stroked the back of my hair, murmuring my name in that dangerous voice of yours. Murmuring, then getting louder and louder as I found a rhythm you liked and began fucking you, using two fingers in your ass, now, and my hand around your cock. You thrust upward with your hips, rising to orgasm, subsiding, and then reaching your peak.

When you finished, you gave me a lazy, kick-back look of pure pleasure, then motioned to a black leather jacket on the back of the door. "Get me one out of my pocket, will you?" you asked, that subtle charm there as always. I would have done anything for you. I stood, on shaky legs, and grabbed your jacket, pawing at it. My hand came out of the inner pocket with a cigar, which I lit and passed to you.

My most treasured image is you on your back, legs still parted, body slicked with sweat, mouth pursed and blowing silvery smoke rings toward the ceiling.

Hot Time in the Old Town

For my birthday, you take me on the most romantic date. The type where I don't have to think about anything, make choices, consider options. It's just you and me, and your preplanned activities, and although I definitely consider myself a feminist, and I know my own mind, I like the surprise of giving up. Of following you blindly through an evening in which all I have to do is wait for the next surprise.

We start the night off at the Mann's Chinese Theater in Hollywood. On our quest for a taste of history, we learn that while most starlets had incredibly small and dainty feet, the spiked heels of my sky-scraper shoes actually fit into several, points sinking into concrete. I imagine being one of the lovely stars, leaning forward to press my hands into the wet sand mixture. The coldness of immortality. You follow my lead, pressing your own large hands into the prints left by screen stars from a generation ago. I notice the size of your hands, and I notice you smile when I make the comparison, but I don't catch onto the fact that you're giving me a clue. Too lost in the glow of being with you, I don't understand that this is an introduction into the pleasures that await.

With a sly sexy smile, you usher me back to the car, and soon we're off and driving again, through the neon brightness of Sunset Boulevard, a pale echo of the famous Vegas strip, maybe, but bright enough for this city girl. I have no idea where you're taking me, but you seem to think I should. In fact, from the comments you make, you seem to believe that if I had been paying closer attention, I'd have gotten the clues by now.

But I'm slow this evening, so that even while you're still talking about the handprints we've just seen, I'm lost in my own world. So pleased to be at your side that I don't even notice where we are when you pull into a high-end sex toy store and park. I look up at the sign, look over at you, and I feel myself grow even more excited. A mix of sweet romance and the sin of dirty sex—you've read my fantasies intimately.

Together, we walk into the store, perusing the items around us with the same sort of intensity that we've just done while playing tourists at the theater. We touch and stroke, ooh and aah, compare sizes and styles. I am aware of the other customers around us, realize that while you and I are dressed for a date, most of the patrons are obviously here on a mission. People don't chitchat; they head directly to one item or another. Why I don't realize you have ulterior motives is beyond me. Usually, I'm not so innocent. Yet I find myself once again a step behind when you make it to the front counter with something in your hand: a serious-looking paddle. Am I slow, or what?

The shopclerk gives us a genuine smile as she rings up your purchase. "Best one on the market," she confides to us. "It's our top-seller." And then she looks directly at me as she says, "Someone's in a for a hot time in the old town tonight."

The girl's right. That someone would most obviously be me. Now, I understand. *Now*, I catch on, and I imagine the handprints you're going to leave behind on my bare bottom before you employ our newly purchased sex toy. I'll be ripe, raw, and red by the time you fuck me—it's all clear now, as clear as handprints immortalized in concrete.

My panties are intensely wet as we exit the store. I could take them off and ring them out, and you'd see a shiny rain of my juices fall onto the dirty asphalt. But I don't. I walk meekly to the car, wait for you to open the door for me, and start to slide inside. Again, you surprise me. Tonight is all about surprises, I suppose. And I think about what you said to me when you picked me up—put yourself in my hands tonight. What you meant was "I'm going to put my hands on you tonight"—which is fine. So fine. Even as you get into the car first, bending me over your lap across the bench seat, slipping my skirt up in the back and caressing my cheeks through my panties. Lowering the panties and spanking that first startling blow against me.

I sigh and squirm, not caring that someone might see, that pedestrians could catch a show of a naughty girl getting her bottom spanked. I think only of the handprints you're leaving behind. Sweet pure handprints on my naked trembling bottom. And I think about the paddle that will kiss my feverish skin when you finish with the introductory open-handed smacks.

When I'm hot and juicy, you reach for the paddle and start to let me have it. There is a warning whistle of the paddle dragging through the air. I suck in my breath at the first blow. This is a completely different experience from being spanked with your open hand. There is no give to the paddle. No caress at the end of a blow. Nothing but the firmness of that sturdy toy against my ripe and ready ass. I can't tell you how much I love it.

Who'd have thought?

You, I realize. You'd have thought. You knew. Before I did. Without me ever having to work through this fantasy aloud. You understood.

In a low voice, you tell me to count for you. Count out loud. I hear myself stutter over the number, but you quickly say, "No. Those were warm-up spanks. We're starting now. If you lose track, we go back to the beginning. So I'm telling you to focus, sweetheart. For your own self-interest. Focus."

And I think about the salesclerk, and realize that she was right—a hot time, in the old town tonight.

The Very Last Time

You're the first thing I notice when I come in the door. I look at you with eyes wide while I wait in line to pay and check my clothes. You're reclining against the far wall, naked except for a pair of boxer shorts. You've been working out; your chest looks good, more developed than when I saw you last, and you've acquired a couple more tattoos.

I'm a little surprised to see you; I didn't realize you came to these things. I feel a churning in the pit of my stomach as I see the second thing I notice: the girl you've got your arm around. God, she's pretty: redheaded and buxom, freckled, with sparkling green eyes I can see from all the way across the room, even in the dim lighting. She's nothing like me, nothing at all. I haven't seen you in two months, and it hurts to see you. And here you are with the prettiest girl in the room, you bastard, while I'm showing up stag.

"Hi, welcome; it's twenty dollars, and please read and sign the release." I stare at the bill, at her, at you, at the girl; the twenty dollars is dull dead weight in my hand, it feels like a one-way ticket to hell. I look back up at you, feeling like I should leave. But then you make eye contact with me; you look shocked, then you smile and wave nervously, turn and say something to the girl you're with.

"Thank you," says the girl behind the table, plucking the twenty from my hand. "Please read and sign the release."

I read, sign, change into my sexy clothes, all the while glancing up to look at you and praying you don't notice me looking. Except that you're looking, every time *I* look. I put on the tight corset, garters, G-string and stockings, heels. I'm decked out, dressed to the nines because I'm coming here alone. I promised myself I would get picked up here—hopefully with a woman. But now I'm frightened, self-conscious, afraid to let myself go. Seeing you here with someone else drives home the fact that we're not together, making our very last time in bed together seem like it was yesterday instead of two months ago.

Maybe I'll just take one quick circuit around the room and leave, make you think that I've evaluated the party and decided it's not cool enough for me. I don't want you to see me having a good time, and I don't know why. More importantly, I don't want you to see me having a *bad* time, if things go wrong and I end up not hooking up with anyone. But mostly I don't want to see *you* having a good time, because you've already won the unspoken contest—you've come here with someone beautiful. And I notice for the zillionth time that she is, indeed, beautiful.

Still, I can't avoid you all night; it's a small room, a small sex party. It hits me, full-force: I've run in to my ex at a sex party. The nightmare of all urban socialites. I have no choice but to make the best of it, because the worst is more than I can handle.

When I walk over to say hello to you, I have to paste the smile on my face—and I almost lose it when I stand in front of you and see that your buxom redhead has her hand in your crotch, on your half-hard cock.

We smile, you stand, we exchange a hug; the feel of your body against mine feels right and wrong at the same time, and I can smell her perfume on you mingled with your sweat. I wish I'd worn perfume of my own so I could send you back to her smelling of me. When you hug me, your hand trails down my back and I think for an instant you're going to cup my ass.

And then it flashes through my mind: Are you going to

ask me to fool around with you and your new girlfriend? After all, we parted on good terms, even if it was entirely your idea and even if you did cheat on me. What if you ask me—will I say yes? That would be the most conspicuous way for me to lose the contest between us, the contest in my own head—you and your pretty girlfriend feel so bad for me that you give me a mercy fuck. Or, worse yet, you think I look good enough for a casual screw, which might be about what I'm worth to you, about what I was always worth.

I pray you don't invite me, but as we chat and you introduce me to her. She gives me a mischievous look that makes me think she's going to invite me to join you. I know I shouldn't, but I know I will say yes, too—just to be there, between you, knowing that you can't touch her without touching me, even if it's for an instant.

In my head, you fuck me, my legs spread around your body as you ride me, your cock thrusting into me as my white body writhes under your tan one, you invading me one more time as your girlfriend and I make out. The image is at once painfully erotic and utterly repulsive; the idea of letting you have me makes me want to be sick, and yet I know I'll do it if you ask, or if she does. I wait for the question, only half admitting to myself that's what I'm waiting for. Which is when the two of you gang up and hand me the coup de grâce: you don't ask.

I give you another hug and walk away shaking, hoping you haven't noticed that I'm disturbed. I head for the refreshment table and find a bottle of water. I sit down next to the table breathing heavily. Guys walk by and nod their heads at me; I'm terrified one of them is going to ask me to play, not because I don't want any of them but because none of them are better looking than you are.

I promised myself I'd find a woman tonight, just a sleazy sex-party pickup to punch my bisexual card. But now I want to find a guy, because it was always your fantasy to see me with another woman, and you never did. Something tells me seeing me fuck another guy might actually make you jealous. But maybe I'm kidding myself. Or maybe it has to be a guy so much better looking than you that you realize how irrelevant you are to me now. That you realize I'm over you, completely and utterly.

I'm still sitting there twenty minutes later when I see the girl coming toward me; slender, late twenties, dark hair cropped in a bob, olive skin. She's wearing tight black leather pants, high boots, and a shimmery black plastic corset that pushes her small tits together into a bit of cleavage. She's gorgeous, and very much your type. I realize with a start that she's packing; her pants bulge in exactly the right place. She comes up to me and introduces herself; her name's Gina. She says she's been watching me and I look blankly at her; I would have been totally incapable of noticing, I think. She asks me if I want to play.

"What did you have in mind?" I ask her.

"I would love to make out with you, give you pleasure."

"And?" My voice is shaking.

"And fuck you really hard."

"I'd like that," I say.

"It's filling up out there," she tells me. "We'd better get a place quick if I'm going to fuck you properly." She takes my hand and my own feels clammy, awkward in her grasp. She gently leads me back out onto the play floor.

And it is filling up: So fast, in fact, that the only free space is a mattress on the floor directly opposite you and your date. And now, to my horror, your date doesn't just have her hand on your crotch. Now she has her head in your lap, your cock out of your bicycling shorts, and her mouth on it, bobbing up and down. You're looking at me, and I'm sure you see my dismay as I watch your girlfriend sucking you.

"How's this?" Gina asks, and I nod.

"Fine," I tell her, frowning.

We slide down onto the clean, starched sheet, and our bodies come together easily. I smell her; she smells like feminine sweat and leather.

"What do you like?" she asks me.

I shrug. "Um... I like to kiss and... um..." I can't find the words, not with you so close.

"You *do* like to get fucked, don't you?" she asks me, her hand resting fetchingly on the bulge in her leather pants.

I nod nervously, and she smiles.

I feel shocked at her bluntness for an instant, feel a gnawing horror in my belly. Then I remember that you asked me the very same thing, in the very same words, on our first date—right after I told you I liked it when men talked dirty to me. I told you yes and you put the information to good use. Very good use. I came three times that first night.

"And your ass?"

I'm left speechless, the memory flooding me.

"Sorry," Gina says. "I guess the polite way to put it is, are you into butt play?" Without knowing why, I shrug; I can't imagine doing that here, in public, with you watching, but to say no would be to let that first fuck from you be a better time than I'm about to have. And I can't bear to let that happen.

Gina kisses me gently on the lips; my eyes stray to you and watch your girlfriend's head bobbing on your cock. Your hand rests lightly on the back of her head, and you watch me with your eyes slightly narrowed. Jealousy? Fascination? Excitement? God, your girlfriend looks good on you, her mane of curly red hair swirling around your belly and thighs as she lavishes attention on your cock. She's got an adorable ass, pretty in a tight little G-string not unlike mine. I wonder if you do to it all the things you used to do to me.

"Distracted?" says Gina, her breath sweet in my face.

I laugh. "Sorry. That's my ex-boyfriend."

"Looks like he's getting some head," she says. "You should return the favor. Would you like that?"

My head feels light; Gina kisses my neck and I nod. "Yes," I say. "I would like that very much."

Her lips find their way down my neck, down my chest; she gently pops my breasts free from the corset and takes each nipple in her mouth in turn, making me squirm as she suckles on them, her teeth gently chewing. "I like that," I tell her. She bites harder and I run my fingers through her hair. She kisses her way down to the bottom of my corset, lets her tongue slide into my belly button, then gently unbuttons my garters and begins to pull my G-string down.

"Mmmmm," she says. "Shaved. Kinky."

"Is... is that okay?" I'm watching her lick your balls, stroking her hand up and down your glistening cock while you watch me.

In answer, she just raises her eyebrows and smiles wickedly. Considerately, she buttons my garters again and slowly kisses her way down my lower belly. I feel her tongue sliding smoothly into my cleft and I gasp, so unused to the feel of a woman's face down there. She teases my clit with her tongue and immediately I feel myself warming up. I lean back on the mattress and spread my legs wide, letting her take control.

God, it feels good. Her tongue is incredible; she knows what she's doing in a way you never did, or never cared to show me. I imagine her going down on your new girlfriend—Desire—as Desire sucks your cock. I moan softly as Gina's tongue works traceries of pleasure up and down my slit.

Now your date pulls her face off your cock, straddles you, and pushes you into her. I watch as your hands come to rest on her ass. She begins to fuck you. Now I can't see your face, just your cock as it slides into her, and the back of your new girlfriend.

I don't know how Gina did it so smoothly, but she got a glove on and lubed up, and slipped two fingers into me, effortlessly. Her tongue works my clit as she fingerfucks me, and I moan. I could come any minute, but she's taking her time, teasing me. Not like your date, who seems to think she's in a porn movie—she's bouncing up and down on you, moaning and throwing her head back, scattering her red hair down her back. I wonder if you told her to show off for me.

Then I don't care, for the first time since I walked in, because Gina's fingertips, three of them, push hard against my G-spot and her other hand, gloved and lubed, slips down between my cheeks and finds my asshole. She's just playing with the outside, but that and her fingers on my G-spot and her tongue on my clit all come together to make me come, and as I moan and grab the mattress she slips one finger into my ass, making me come harder, making me scream. I can't stop myself; I scream loud, like I always do when I come that hard. I hear scattered applause and feel a wicked sense of accomplishment. But there's no time for that, or for wondering if you heard me come and felt jealous, because Gina strips off her gloves and begins to unzip her leather pants to pull her cock out.

I put my legs up over her shoulders, my knees cocked just so, and she penetrates me smoothly, quickly. Her cock is huge, a big swollen head and thick silicone shaft that makes my pussy, so sensitive from its recent orgasm, quiver and convulse. I guess Gina never read the "size doesn't matter" chapter of the lesbian sex manual. I'm going to come again, I know it, and Gina's going to make me do it whether I want to or not. She makes eye contact as her hips pump her cock into me, and she reaches down to caress my breasts as I look into her eyes, riveted. God, she feels good inside me. When my eyes flicker down and I try to see what you're up to—but the angle isn't right, I can't see a thing, Gina laughs, slides her cock out of me, and slaps my thigh.

"You like watching him? Why don't we turn you around. That way you can 'know' you're getting it better than he is."

She guides me onto all fours, my ass in the air and my legs spread. She mounts me from behind and slides her cock into me, filling me with her. She reaches under me and rubs my clit while she fucks me, and it's a good minute before I even look up to see what you're doing. You've got your date in the same position Gina has me, and you're fucking her from behind while you look at me, your eyes staring daggers. But then our eyes meet, and you smile, sheepishly, as if I know exactly what you're doing. And I don't care, because Gina's cock in my pussy is going to make me come. Then I do come, screaming, not because I want to impress you but because it feels so fucking good. I pound back onto her as her hand rubs my clit, molding onto me until she's sure I've finished coming. Your redhead looks like she's fallen asleep on her hands and knees, methodically bouncing back against you as if in a trance. I can see you're only half-hard. Suddenly I feel guilty, like I've ruined your evening, like I've taken away that hard cock I used to love so much.

I'm so lost in my thoughts that I don't even realize Gina is continuing to fuck me, still rubbing my clit. I've already come twice and at first I don't know if I can do it again. But as I feel the length of her cock sliding deeper into me, I hear myself shrieking in pleasure and I know I'm going to come sooner or later.

Gina starts fucking me slowly at first, until I thrust myself back onto her cock, forcing it into me hard. She's still got her hand on my clit, and I reach down to guide it, pushing her fingers onto me harder as we pump our bodies together. And there, before I know it, I come a third time, opened wide on a strange woman's cock. I squirm and writhe and shudder with her cock inside me, and as my eyes come slowly open again I stare out at you, my body aching with the afterglow of release, and I realize I've done it: I came more often than you ever made me come in a single fuck. For some reason that seems both exhilarating and creepy.

But you and your redhead are packing up to go, and you have a bitter look on your face. Your date looks annoyed. I wonder if you came. I'm sure you didn't. That sends another spasm of pleasure through my body, and I have to take a deep breath. Oh God, I hurt you. I really hurt you. I made you jealous, I kept you from properly fucking your girlfriend. I'm a bad person. But I came so hard.

Gina pulls out and guides me onto my side on the now-soaked sheet. She wipes the lube off of my thighs and her cock, tucks it back into her pants, gets up and brings me a glass of juice. I sip the juice as Gina cuddles up behind me, her cock pushing through her leather pants. You and your date are over in the corner, both of you with sour faces, arguing.

"Did you have a better time than he did?" asks Gina.

"Yes, I think so." And it makes me sad, really sad.

"Good for you," she says, kisses me one last time, and stands up. She blows me a kiss and drifts away—off to find her girlfriend? Boyfriend? Another casual fuck she can make come three times and totally erase any sense of lingering romantic feeling for an old flame?

Long moments pass as men drift by me, nod, throw predatory glances over my splayed legs. I smile and nod, and they pass me by, one by one as I enjoy their lust. I evaluate their faces, knowing I could eat any one of them for lunch.

Until I see one I couldn't eat for lunch—or, maybe, one I just did.

You sit down next to me, still wearing your boxer shorts,

your upper half clad in a tight tank top.

"Hi," you say.

"Hi." I don't look at you, suddenly ashamed.

"You look great."

"Thanks," I say.

"Did you have fun with that girl...."

"Gina," I say, as if telling you her name makes her more real—makes the fuck more real. "Yeah, I had a great time."

There's an awkward silence, broken when you blurt out: "Listen, I've been thinking about you a lot, and—"

I surprise myself with how quickly I spring into action, to put a stop to the processing before it starts. "Look, if this is going to be one of those let's-talk-about-our-friendship moments, it's the wrong place. Haven't you ever heard of a coffee shop?"

It's so mean I'm amazed. I'm never that mean. And I immediately feel guilty, seeing the hurt in your eyes as you stare into mine, wondering things you shouldn't be wondering.

But it all stops when you bend forward and I feel your lips on mine. I don't pull away, but I don't respond; I just let you kiss me, your tongue sliding into my mouth. I can taste her, your redhead, mingled with the mouthwash you must have just sampled in the bathroom—did you plan this, and think it would be polite to sweep away the remnants of her before you came on to me?

"What happened to your date?" I ask bitterly when our lips part. My head is spinning; your kiss took my breath away, just like it did two months ago when we made love the very last time.

"She's gone," you say. "We were a casual thing, anyway. She's got a boyfriend in Santa Fe." You're leaning against me, your hand on my thigh, dangerously close to my pussy, which aches in response to your proximity. I'm hungry for you. I hate it, but I'm hungry for you.

"Is she pissed?"

"Yeah," you laugh. "Thanks."

"Always glad to be of service."

And you kiss me again; this time, I don't go limp. Instead, my tongue meets yours and we kiss desperately, like it really is the very last one, and I realize in the flash of an instant that I don't want it to be, that I can't bear it to be. I feel your hand moving up my thigh.

"What are you doing?" I moan softly.

"I'm going to fuck you," you say. "Please don't say no. I think I'd go crazy if you say no."

"You're already crazy, for doing this," I say.

"I know," you tell me, and our lips meet again, our tongues tangling as I feel your hand against my pussy, your fingers finding my clit easily. I moan. I want this, and however hard I try, I'm not going to stop wanting it. So I just want it, and I push my body against yours, reaching for your cock.

It comes free from your shorts easily, and wrapping my hand around it seems the most natural thing in the world. Your fingers slip into me and I stroke your cock, pushing you onto the mattress and laying beside you as you kiss my neck. Your cock slips out of my grasp as you move down my body. Your tongue traces its path over my shoulders, over my breasts, pausing to tug my nipples free from the corset, taking each nipple in your mouth and suckling it gently. You know from experience that that's the quickest way to get me going. But you don't have to get me going; Gina already did that for you, fucking me silly in full view of you and your date. And even if she hadn't, the smell and taste of you would render my body explosively reactive to your touch.

You linger on my thighs, kissing and sucking, teasing me before letting your mouth mold to my cunt. My back arches and my ass lifts high off the mattress as I claw the threadbare sheets. I feel your tongue on my clit and I know, just know in my bones that there's no way I'm going to come—that would make it four times, absolutely unheard of for me. Except that your tongue works wonders, its familiar surface conjuring sensations in my clit that I never knew existed. No one's ever licked me after three orgasms. I've never *had* three orgasms before. I want to push you away, but as you center on my clit and push me further, I can't bear to let go of the sensation, let go of you.

I put my hands on your face, pull you away from my cunt, look into your saddened eyes.

"Fuck me," I tell you.

You strip off your tank top and boxer shorts, and your tattooed body rises glorious between my legs. I spread my thighs as far as they will go, my cunt feeling like a hungry mouth ready to eat up your cock. When you touch the head of it to me, I want it more than I've ever wanted anything. I feel it going in and I throw my head back and moan.

It hurts me, a little, my cunt so sensitive after being fucked so hard by Gina. But the faint irritation goes away in moments as you sink into me, the shape of your cock so familiar and comforting. You settle your naked body down on top of me and hold me close as I wrap my arms and legs around you and pull you into my grasp.

"Fuck me," I repeat. There's a small crowd watching us, getting their voyeuristic thrill, with no idea of what's really going on. This is the stupidest thing I've ever done, giving myself to you, taking you back inside me after our break-up. But I wouldn't dream of stopping it. It's the most divine feeling in the world. You start to fuck me rhythmically, following my moans as a guide. I know from experience when you're fucking to come and when you're fucking to pleasure me, and this time it's all about my pleasure. And it's working—I'm on the edge of orgasm within minutes, whispering in your ear that I love you.

I'll kick myself later, but in the very last kiss I couldn't stop it from coming out, and believe it or not I meant it.

You fuck me faster as I come, as I writhe and moan under you. Now I can sense the change in your motions—you're close yourself, and you're going to come inside me. "Come for me," I beg you as my own orgasm echoes through my naked body. "Please. Come inside me." You let out a sigh and I feel your body tense, then release as you let yourself go inside me. My pussy floods with your come and it's the most reassuring feeling in the world.

Maybe, or maybe not, because in the last kiss before you come, you say "I love you, too," your voice strained with the effort of orgasm, and whether you mean it or not, it's perfect, like a moment from the sleaziest romance novel ever written, like the greeting card of the shameless hussy, surrounded by a small crowd of naked, cheering men.

I guess it's a little bit surprising to me when, as we're pulling on our clothes, you take me in your arms and say it. Have I been wanting it, wanting to hear you say it? I guess I have, without even knowing it. Not "I love you"—I've already got that.

"Want to get a bite to eat?"

I pull away from you, look you in the eye, frowning.

"Are you asking me for a date?" I say solemnly.

"Yes," you say. "Absolutely." Then, thinking better of it, you add: "Maybe a really strange one."

I watch your eyes for a moment, and then I smile. Then I kiss you, and I know for the first time this evening that it's *not* the very last kiss we'll share, that this was not the last time we'll make love. Our last time will come some days, weeks, years in the future—who knows? The very last time is a sacred one, and to my surprise we haven't reached it yet.

You Don't Know Me

You think you know me, but you don't. I can see from the slightly smug look in your eyes that you have me pegged as one of those shy wallflower type of girls. Bookish. Smart. Hell, smarter than you, anyway. At least, you've got that part right. And I'll bet that when you shut your eyes and picture what I've got on underneath my skirt, you think white or pastel, plain cotton briefs. Maybe you find that a little bit sexy, the thought of something so innocent. Maybe the image gives you a thrill, but you shouldn't get too lost in the vision because you're wrong.

Face it, you don't know me.

And just to let you in on a little secret: I don't wear pastels. Not ever.

Still, you think you know me. And sure, you know *parts* of me. For instance, you know that I have the answers to all of your questions. That's my job, and I do it well. I work in research, and when you need something, and you need it yesterday, I'm the first person you come to. If I don't have the answer in my head, I'll get your information by the end of the hour. I'm good. I know how to make a library work for me. I also know that you talk to your buddies about me, joking about how all I need is a raucous session between the sheets to melt my frozen core. Or, to put it the way you might, "A long hard ride on a steady rod."

But you're wrong.

Because you don't know me.

If you did, you'd know exactly what I need. I wouldn't have to spell it out. I wouldn't have to give you the rules, the precise restrictions that you must follow if you're going to be with me. But because you don't know, because you can't even begin to understand, I'll give you more than a clue. I'll tell you exactly what I need.

Picture this: you, on my bed, the very edge of my bed, looking up at me with a humble expression on your handsome face, waiting patiently for my next command. I'm standing in front of you, wearing my finest black corset, the ties perfectly laced, my back perfectly straight. I've got on fishnets and spiked heels, and my long dark hair is down instead of contained neatly in a bun. It's straight and thick and it shines in the light from several well-placed candles. You've never seen me like this before. Not in real life. Not in your fantasies. Now, things are starting to be clearer in your head. You understand how massively you misjudged me. You understand that you had it all wrong before, but at this juncture in time, *before* no longer matters. All that matters is now.

I look at you, see that you're trying to behave, that the rules I gave you earlier in the evening are throbbing in your head. How can you do precisely what I want you to, when your own wants are growing more urgent by the second? All you want is to spread me out on the mattress and do those things to me that you told the boys about on the third floor. Melt my core.

But it takes a lot to melt me.

I run the tip of my crop under your chin, making you lift your head up and tighten your jaw. I tell you what to do next, and my voice is cold and calm and even. When you speak, your own voice has changed. Your usually strong timbre has slipped to one of almost a whisper. A hiss in the air, like smoke.

Yes, Mistress.

That's right, I want to say. That's my boy. But I don't have to say a word. I simply act. Because actions can resonate. I don't have to tell you to behave. I can make you behave. With a combination of power and intensity and a small, clear spark of true pain. You do what I want. You are the one to sprawl out on the bed, belly down, cock pressed against the mattress. You wait while I walk around the bed, observing you, and you hold still when I trace the crop once again along your skin. But now, the tip of the weapon is probing you. Touching your balls between your thighs, dragging down the crack between your asscheeks.

I am enjoying every moment of your torment. I know that you are scared, and that makes me hotter still. I know that despite your fears, you're more aroused than you've ever been. Giving in is your secret fantasy. Letting you give in is mine.

I'm not going to destroy you tonight. Don't worry. I'm only going to set things clear for the future. We have plenty of time to get to know each other better. Tonight, I'm only interested in putting you in your place and showing you how hard you'll come from submitting.

The crop is just a tool tonight, a way to make you tremble. I tease you with it until you start to moan, and I let you have a few gentle taps on your naked ass, showing you that you won't try to hide from being my good boy. Instead, you'll raise up and meet each and every blow.

Then I set it down and I come onto the bed with you. I have you roll over and I use my hand to jack your cock. I work you forcefully, at just the right pace. I drizzle lube over you and you groan at how good that feels. The warmth of my skin heats the oily lubrication and you start to buck and moan. There is a strangeness to you of being naked and played with while I am still dressed and in charge. I can see in your eyes that you are trying to work this out. You'd have thought I'd be the one moaning, right? But no. Not right now.

Right now, I just want to pump you, my fist working, while I gaze at you in my steely way and wait for your pleasure.

"Not yet," I tell you. "Not yet." But you can't wait.

Even as you come, come hard and fast against my fingers, disobeying me when you simply can't obey any longer, I smile to myself. I have so many plans for you, ways to take you higher, endlessly higher, to push your limits forever. And you have no idea—because you don't know me.

While She Was Dancing

I won't tell her if you don't.

It was a mistake, right? It's not as if we *meant* for it to happen. Well....at least, you didn't.

I guess I did, sort of. Not before, but during. At least, I let it happen. I knew what was happening. I didn't plan it or anything, but.... I knew what was happening, while it was happening—and I let it happen anyway.

So I'll admit it. I'm the bad one. You were just disoriented, I don't know; maybe you were a little drunk, too. And horny. Really, really horny. And hard. Really, really hard. So hard I'm not 100% sure I'm even going to be able to walk today. Which is kind of a good thing....

I won't tell her. You won't tell her. So she'll never ever know. It'll be our little secret. One I'll never, ever tell *anyone*.

But I'll remember it. I'll think about it. Look, I'm not going to lie to you. I'm going to think about it a lot. A whole lot.

A whole, whole lot.

I was turned on, see? Whenever she goes away, I get really turned on. I get wet, like, immediately, before she even closes the door. I know I'm going to have the room all to myself, with plenty of privacy to do....things. I have some lingerie, just a little, and I keep it hidden under my mattress. It gets kind of wrinkled, so I have to smooth it out. But it still looks good when it goes on me. It's not much—just a little tiny thong and a camisole that only comes halfway down my stomach, revealing my belly. It looks really good on my breasts; it makes the nipples stand out, peaked, and they're always hard when I'm looking at myself in that outfit.

That's how it started, anyway. I'm not like she is; I don't have the guts to go into Kitten's Top Drawer or wherever and buy any really sexy lingerie. But I've seen hers, and she's been in those stores, I can tell. I've seen her underwear drawer. You know, the weekends when she wasn't there. The weekends I was alone.

She's got some really sexy lingerie.

So that's what happened last night.

You don't know this, but she left for the weekend. You know that friend of hers from the city? The one who's all hooked in with these awesome, famous DJs from Europe and stuff? At the last minute she got passes to this really exclusive club where some really hot DJ was playing. You know how much she likes dancing, right? Yeah, of course you do. She loves to dance. She looks really sexy dancing. Anyway, she got these passes to this special club. She's going to be gone all weekend, and that's why she wasn't here last night. She had to go right away to make it on time, and her cell phone was out of juice, so she couldn't call you. She asked me to tell you.

Whoops. Guess I forgot.

I'd tried on a couple of her things before, you know, without asking. She would have loaned me almost anything, but the stuff she kept in her bottom drawer would probably have been going too far. So I didn't ask. I just slipped it out of there and I put it on—the whole outfit, as if I was getting dressed to go out. Go out somewhere really slutty, like a strip club or something. You couldn't see it last night because it was dark, but I'm sure you've seen it on her before, some time in good light. I'm sure she left the lights on and showed it off for you. Maybe she even danced for you, the way I was dancing for myself before you showed up. The whole outfit is pink and white, kind of virginal but really slutty because it's so skimpy, so lacy, so see-through. I had never seen her in it, but I could imagine, and I bet it looks incredible on her.

I put on a bunch of makeup, that bright red lipstick of hers that she says is called "cocksucker red." She says you always want head when she wears that color. Probably because she tells you it's called that. I put on eye shadow, too, that cheesy '80s blue eye shadow she wears when she's going out dancing, painting it on thick and tawdry. I looked myself over in the full-length mirror on the back of the door. God, I looked like a tart. Like a stripper or something. The bra is a push-up bra; she's a little less busty than me so the bra squeezed tight and made my tits look two sizes bigger than they are. They looked all perky and inviting the way the padding held them.

Then there was her sexy pink garter belt, white stockings, matching pink and white G-string with an embroidered rose at the top. The G-string part is so, so skimpy. I can't believe she would ever wear it out. The little V that dips down where the rose is sits just like an inch above my pussy. I put the G-string on over my garters, so I could take it off without taking the garter belt off. But then, you already know that part.

See, I guess I had kind of planned it, because I'd seen this outfit in her underwear drawer before. Maybe that's why I shaved when I took a shower yesterday morning. I mean, shaved all the way—my pussy was smooth. So maybe I *did* kind of plan to try it on. All day yesterday I liked the way it felt, rubbing bare against my tight jeans because I hadn't worn anything under them. I would just die if anyone knew I'd shaved down there.

But now you know, I guess. You found out last night.

It's not like I've got a boyfriend, not like her. So there's no one to see it; it's just for my own pleasure. I like it smooth down there...but now you know. Now you know everything.

You know I shave my pussy and you know what I feel like inside. God, I'm getting wet just remembering it.

It was early, like eleven. I ran my hands all over my body, touching the smooth satin and the lace where it caressed my breasts, my belly, my hips, my pussy. There was music outside, a big loud party, everyone getting really drunk. I didn't want to join the party, though; I was having too much fun by myself.

So I turned on music, loud, really loud—like they'd play in a club. You know that CD she has? *American Music to Strip To* or something? Really hard, grinding stuff with lots of women moaning. Lots of guitar, heavy, heavy drums, thick bass....when she plays that album, I always get turned on, even if she's sitting, like, right there. I always get wet.

So I played it loud. That's when I put on that skirt I was wearing. I've seen her wear it lots of times, and I was always kind of jealous. It comes down so low on her hips you can totally see her thong sticking out of it. It's so short that she flashes everyone if she stands up too fast—I mean, like, full-on, not just a little glimpse if she's careless.

But you already knew I tried it on, because you took it off of me last night. You slid it off me and fucked me. I guess you're the reason I picked that skirt of hers to try on. Because she told me how all she has to do is put that skirt on, and you fuck her good.

She also told me what you did to her the first time she wore it for you. How she found herself out on the bridge, bent over, in the middle of the night, you pulling the skirt up to her waist and just giving it to her, hard, so hard she came, like, right away and then came again before you shot your wad, not even caring if people could hear her. Yup, she told me. She told me about how you pulled the skirt up so high it ripped and she had to sew it, and how you spanked her and called her little girl and bit the back of her neck and kept talking dirty and all sorts of nasty things like that. God, I got so incredibly wet when she told me about that. I always thought you were so cute, I guess, so maybe that's why I got really turned on, but I bet she looked really good, too, bent over the railing on the bridge with her ass in the air and her legs spread. She told me how she screamed when she came the second time. And the third. You didn't know about the third time, probably. She was embarrassed, because it was when you were spanking her. She came really hard. I shouldn't have told you that. She was embarrassed to tell you that she came from being spanked, but she did. God, I think about that a lot.

In fact, I think about that story a lot—like, all the time. I come all the time thinking about how good you fucked her on the bridge. That's why I put that skirt on. That's why I put on the little crop top she was wearing that night you fucked her on the bridge, the one you pulled up so you could feel her tits while you gave it to her from behind. The crop top that says "Porn Star," which is kind of what she was that night, since she told me about it and now she stars in so many of my fantasies, bent over the railing, getting fucked by you while you feel her tits. I love that top on her; it looks great. It totally shows her nipples, remember? Because she wears it without a bra. Her nipples just stick right out, even if they're not that hard, but it seems like they're always hard when she wears that shirt. She told me she likes guys looking at them. You remember how sexy she looks with that top on, nipples poking out telling the whole world she's wet 'cause guys are looking at her? Of course you remember. You're probably always looking at her nipples whenever she wears it, I guess. I'm always looking, too. Sometimes it's hard for me to take my eyes off them.

It shows mine, too. My nipples, I mean. Even though I was wearing a bra, it was tight and thin over my nipples, holding my breasts up, pushing them against the tight cotton. Like I said, I'm a little bustier than her, so the crop top was really tight and kind of pulled across my breasts, not really going much below them. Showing my whole belly. I thought that looked really sexy. I thought the whole thing looked really sexy, especially with the white lace tops of her stockings showing on my thighs, under the hem of the skirt, reminding me how incredibly short the skirt was and reminding me that I was wearing that slutty garter belt. I really looked good. You couldn't see me because it was dark, but I looked really, really good.

I looked especially good as I started dancing for myself, pretending I was a stripper, giving myself a little private dance. I started to get really wet as I saw how good I looked. I started to feel my clit throb. I ran my hands over my body and pulled up the skirt, showing the G-string and my shaved pussy. I ran my fingertips over the place where the skirt had been mended, remembering how you pulled it up so hard it ripped, how you yanked on it, you were so eager to get your cock inside her. That made me really hot, feeling that rip, actually touching it. I moved with the music, wondering what I would feel like if there was someone there watching me. I looked at my body shimmying and writhing, tried to make my moves sexier, sluttier, more provocative. I looked good. I looked really, really hot.

I looked so hot I kind of lost control.

I got my vibrator out from under my mattress and turned around with my back to the mirror, bending over so I could see the skirt riding up on my ass, showing the pink lace panties. I pulled the skirt up and spread my legs a little, watching as I tugged the G-string out of the way.

Then I started fucking myself.

I don't turn the vibrator on when I fuck myself with it, see, I just like the shape. I like the way it's hard against the inside of my pussy, that spot right up from the inside that always makes me come. That's called the G-spot. You know you hit it last night, you hit it perfectly. Something about the way your cock's shaped, I guess. It surprised me, but you hit it dead on, every thrust. I'm getting so wet telling you this.

I was bent way over by then and fucking myself from behind, looking over my shoulder so I could watch my ass in the mirror as it swayed back and forth, pretending that I was pushing myself onto a cock instead of pushing a vibrator into me.

I was really close to coming, like, right away. I was so close I had to stop, because I didn't want to come yet. I wanted to dance some more. I moved with the music, feeling it pulse through me. I was so, so wet. I would have fucked just about anyone who walked through that door. No offense.

I started to get all sweaty, dancing in the little room. The crop top started to get a little soaked. That's why I did what I did next. I went over to her nightstand and got out her perfume. I don't wear perfume, see. And I was....well, to tell the truth I was kind of turned on pretending to be her. She's really sexy, you know? Of course you know. You know exactly how sexy she is.

So I lifted my face, pointed the mister, and misted.

I think I put on a little too much. It smelled strong. But it made me smell like her. I danced some more and got more and more excited. I really wished I had a big mirror by the bed so I could spread my legs and fuck myself in that sexy outfit and watch it as I penetrated my pussy with the vibrator. But I didn't, and if there was one thing I wanted just then, it was to get fucked. So I went over and got on my bed.

The vibrator went in easy, hard plastic against the inside of my pussy. Pushing up against my G-spot. I could hear myself moaning, so loud I was afraid I was going to alert the neighbors even over the pounding music. I was going to come any minute, and I wasn't sure I wanted to just yet. I liked fucking myself. I wanted to fuck myself as hard as I could.

Which is how it occurred to me, I guess.

Yeah. She did. She told me everything.

I mean, she gave me the details. Don't worry, I'm not grossed out. I think it's kind of cool. I think it's kind of sexy that she likes it that way. I mean, it's slutty, I guess, but in a good way. Like, brave. Audacious. Sexy.

I wanted it that way, too. Just like she gets it.

I knew enough to know you had to use something to make it go in easier. Yeah, well, I didn't have any. I mean, when I put that vibrator inside me I never need any kind of lube. I'm always so wet it just goes right in all the way before I even know what's happening. But it's not like I've ever put it in *there*. It's not like I've *ever* put anything there.

Well, now I have.

But last night, I hadn't.

She has all this lube in her lingerie drawer. I'd seen it when I was looking through. Really big bottles, I mean really, really big, like a pint or something, you know? Of course you know, you do it to her all the time.

I wanted to do it, I mean, I wanted to just try it. I wanted to put something in there, and I was so turned on I knew I could do it.

So I got back on my bed and rolled over on my belly and put my butt in the air and uncapped the lube.

I reached back and poured a little onto my butt...it didn't seem like enough. So I poured a little more, reached back and rubbed it in. I put some on the tip of the vibrator. Kind of a big wet glob. I reached back awkwardly and got ready to push it in.

I got it in, all right—about an inch. It felt good. I mean, really, really good. Yeah, I guess you know that. I guess you know I like it that way. Well, it caught me off-guard. My whole body sort of shook and I felt like I was going to come right away.

Which is how it happened—I mean, it was carnage. Total carnage.

Lube *everywhere.*

I was totally freaked out—I mean, it was stupid, but I was just so embarrassed. I don't even know where to buy that stuff. I had wasted all her lube and now she was going to find out, plus my bed was now a rapidly growing puddle of goo, right in the middle where I was supposed to sleep. And it's not like my bed is really wide enough for me to sleep over on the side.

I was so mad at myself. I felt really embarrassed. I mean, I figured I was really in trouble.

The towels didn't do anything. Like, anything at all. The lube just kept spreading, soaking through my sheets and making my mattress totally soggy. I knew I should have used a mattress pad. Once I had used every towel in the place to wipe up the lube, my bright idea to sleep on a pile of towels was pretty much not going to happen.

So....well, I mean, it's not like she was going to be using hers, right?

And I was so freaked out it's not like I was going to get off now. I mean, I would *never* masturbate on her bed. Never.

I was really tired after a full hour of trying to mop up lube from my bed. I was feeling guilty and stupid, and even though my pussy was totally aching, I was too freaked out to try to come any more.

So I just let it go. But I didn't want to undress. I was exhausted, and besides, I liked having these clothes on.

I was going to have to wash them anyway—so I just stretched, kicked off her high-heeled fuck-me-pumps. Took one last look at myself, at how good I looked in the full-length mirror. I blew myself a kiss.

And crawled into her bed.

I love the way she smells. Not just her perfumes and soaps and stuff, but the way her *body* smells. I guess you probably do, too. It's all musky and sexy and sometimes it just sort of turns me on, smelling her when it's just the two of us or even when she's not here, when I can smell her on her sheets and clothes and stuff.

Okay, I'll admit it. I've smelled her clothes. Not a lot or anything, but just sometimes when I needed that extra turn-on. She smells really good, doesn't she. Sexy.

So I just lay there in her bed with the lights out, getting more and more turned on. I really wanted to come. But I felt weird about the lube thing, so I just figured I'd go to sleep.

It took me a long time, like at least an hour, laying there, smelling her, thinking about her, thinking about you. Thinking about the two of you doing it in this bed, where I was trying to sleep. Thinking about you doing...*that* to her.

I touched my pussy a little as I drifted off to sleep. Just to see if I was still wet. I was. Really, really wet. It felt good to touch it, but I knew I shouldn't take it too far. I knew I shouldn't come.

Then I finally managed to get to sleep, and I fell *hard*. You know when you fall really, really deeply asleep all of a sudden? This was like that. When I woke up I had no idea where I was or what that noise was over by the window.

I saw your leg come in, saw your body follow it. You pulled the window closed and locked it.

It was dark. Really, really dark. The lights outside go off at 2:30, you know. I guess it's to save power. So neither of us could see anything.

You're considerate, I guess. You're a gentleman. I heard you tiptoe over to my bed and lean over it. I still didn't remember who I was or where I was or what I was doing there, but thinking back I guess you were checking to make sure I wasn't there.

I heard you pat my pillow, just to make sure.

Then I heard your zipper go down.

You took off all your clothes. I started to come to my senses as I listened to you undress.

Then I heard your footsteps, soft now as you tiptoed.

I felt your body, sliding under the covers. Naked.

I'll admit it. The second I felt that touch, I wanted it. I wanted you to fuck me. At first I didn't know who I was, if I was her or me, if I was in her bed or mine—if you were her boyfriend or mine. Then, when I felt your body naked against mine, I didn't care.

I was on my back, and I felt your weight on top of me. You're a big guy, and you felt heavy—sexy, hard, imposing. My pussy would have been wet instantly, even if it wasn't before.

You put your face against my neck and took a big, deep breath of me, smelling her perfume. Maybe smelling her scent from her pillow, from her sheets and blankets. I don't know. Whatever it was, you didn't hesitate.

You kissed me.

I felt your tongue going in my mouth, teasing me open. I felt my nipples stiffen instantly. I felt my pussy go wet and throbbing, throbbing so hard, that I would have done anything, pretended to be *anybody,* to get a cock inside it. And I could feel your cock against me, hard already, pressing on my belly as you kissed me.

I whimpered softly, feeling my nipples harden fully against your naked chest. You knew exactly what I was wearing, knew exactly how to take it off of me.

You lifted the crop top and pulled down the bra.

You started suckling on my nipples.

One word. I could have said one word and it would have been over, you would have known I wasn't her. But I bit my lip, didn't even let myself moan for fear you'd recognize that, too. Not that you've ever heard me moan....well, now you have. Now you've heard me moan a lot.

So I just held totally still, felt the electric touch of your lips and tongue on my nipples. Felt your teeth close gently around them, biting me a little.

She likes that, I know. She told me she likes it a lot. Sometimes it can almost make her come. I like it, too, but I've never told anyone that before. I didn't even tell her that when she told me *she* likes it. I just blushed and looked away. I think she likes telling me things that make me blush.

My arms went around your shoulders, and I cradled your head against me. You sucked harder, using your hand to gently pinch and knead my other nipple, while your free hand went down my body.

You felt the skirt and said softly, "Fuck, I love it when you wear this skirt."

You kissed me then, hard, your tongue going deep inside me. Your cock was really hard against my stomach. It felt really big, a little scary. As you kissed me, I felt you pulling up my skirt.

You took hold of the G-string and pulled it down.

I just lay there, immobile, paralyzed, as you slipped the G-string down my stockinged thighs and over my ankles. I couldn't see, but I heard you take a deep breath.

"God, I love the way your pussy smells," you said.

That's when I started moaning, because I couldn't stop myself. You were kissing your way back up my body, up my stockings and then around the lace tops, savoring them.

Then you went to work on my thighs.

Your tongue traced circles closer and closer to my pussy.

That's when I think I passed the point of no return. I really should have said something. I don't know what. Maybe, um, "Don't go down on me, I'm not your girlfriend...."

But I didn't.

Instead, I slowly spread my legs as far as they would go.

The first touch of your tongue on my clit made my whole body convulse, my mouth go wide open, made me claw at the sheets that smelled like her. I stuffed my hand in my mouth and bit down to keep from screaming, it felt so good. It was like I had the vibrator on my clit, like I had it inside me a moment ago, like I was tottering on the brink of orgasm and you came in to push me over the edge.

"You shaved," you said from between my legs, your voice dark and husky with want. "You know I've been wanting that. Thank you. God, your pussy is so sexy shaved."

Your tongue descended on my clit again and a pathetic little whimper came out of my stuffed-full mouth, my body twisting and writhing on you.

When you pulled up, you said "I'm going to fuck you so fucking good tonight. I'm going to show you how much I appreciate your doing this for me. Getting all shaved and dressed up for me. You are such a fucking slut and I fucking love it, baby. God, I'm going to fuck you until you scream. You're not going to be able to walk for three days, baby."

That's all it took. Just hearing that from your lips was enough to drive me over the edge, but it took the next firm touch of your tongue to really do it. I came so hard, my hand coming away from my mouth and great shuddering sobs of pleasure coming out of my wide-open mouth. I think I came harder than I'd ever come before....though, not since.

You didn't stop, either. You kept eating me hungrily, like you were desperate for the taste of my pussy, desperate for the feel of its shaved smoothness against your face. I totally lost control. I writhed on the bed and grabbed the pillows and punched them as hard as I could, as I came and came and came, and you didn't stop until I was whimpering "Please....please....please...." in a little tiny voice, not even able to beg you to stop the pleasure because it overwhelmed me so much. I was totally under your control, helpless on your mouth as you devoured me. I didn't even worry that you'd know who I was, and I guess my voice sounded enough like hers that you didn't realize it. That's when your mouth came away from my pussy and I heard you shifting on the bed, felt the weight of you on top of me.

And I realized it was going to happen.

You were going to fuck me.

I guess I could have stopped then, but there was nothing left of my mind, really. I was just this twisting mass of lust, under you on the bed, wanting your cock so bad I would have told you I was Eleanor Roosevelt if it would have gotten you to put that cock inside me.

I've had sex before; it's not like I'm a virgin. But I don't know if you know this, but you're really, really big. You have a huge, huge cock. Especially the head. It's so thick that if I had time to think about it I never would have let you put it inside me. I mean, even if you weren't her boyfriend. I already knew you were huge, I mean, she told me—she tells me everything—she told me how she had to get used to it, how she had to try hard to take it at first. But now she loves it.

I loved it right away, even though I felt that first wave of fear when I realized it was going to happen, when I felt the push of your head against my pussy, felt it sliding up and down between my swollen lips, felt it thick against my entrance. You're used to fucking her, though, and I know she likes it fast and hard—not too much foreplay, not too much teasing, just right in, deep, all the way.

That's how you gave it to me.

But I guess I'm smaller than her, you know, down there. Your head pushed into me and my back arched and—don't get me wrong—it felt so good, so incredible, but I thought at first it was going to rip me in two. I would have stopped you if I could have.

But I couldn't. Because I was still coming.

I mean, not really coming, right in the middle of it. But there were still these spasms going through my body, and it felt like I was going to come again. My pussy was so sensitive, so incredibly sensitive, and clenching so tight from such an intense climax, that it didn't want to accept you.

Besides, it's not like I have a boyfriend. It's not like I'm used to it, really. The last time I had sex was a year ago, and I guess I never really did it all that much anyway. Certainly not with a guy as big as you.

So when the head of your cock popped into me, my mouth went open wide and I reached down, instinctively, my palms spreading against your chest. Not that I wanted you to go out, but my instinct, my reflex, was that I couldn't take it, there was no way I could take it, and so I started to push you away.

I guess she likes it kind of rough. I mean, I knew that. I know about the cuffs and how she really likes you to hold her wrists. But it still caught me off-guard, totally.

You grabbed my wrists and shoved them down against the bed, leaning forward, your weight holding me down, bearing me into the bed. Then you shoved your cock into me, hard, so fucking hard I thought I was going to explode. I thought I was so stuffed full of your cock that the top of my head would pop off. And you didn't stop there, either.

I guess you like that, too. Like it kind of rough. Like holding her down a little, I mean, nothing too kinky, but I know you do it that way a lot. I know you hold her down and fuck her really hard. Really, really hard.

That's what you did to me, while I was under you, spread and helpless, held down by your weight and your hands on my wrists, forcing them against the mattress, forcing me to take you. I knew that if I opened my mouth, if I spoke one word, the truth would be out. And imagine how it felt when I remembered about that seminar you went to. About the safewords and stuff. And I realized I didn't know her safeword, that nothing I could say would stop you, that I was totally, utterly out of control and, for all intents and purposes, I was yours.

And that's what's really surprising.

Because that's when I came.

Hard. I don't just mean like a continuation of the orgasm I had before, you know, which happens when I'm masturbating sometimes with the vibrator. I mean like a whole new orgasm, on a whole new level. I came so hard as you pounded your cock into me that I swear I must have passed out for a moment. I was just lost in the sensations of your cock violating me, in the feeling of you holding me down on the bed.

I mean, she explained it to me, explained everything. You can always say "safeword," right? So why didn't I say it? Or, I mean, I could have just said your name, you would have recognized my voice, known I wasn't her.

But I didn't. I guess because I didn't want to.

As the sensations began to fade, as the most intense orgasm of my life echoed through my lingerie-clad body underneath your rutting, naked one, I heard you say it. "You're so incredibly tight tonight," I heard you growling roughly, insensitive, callous. "Are you a fucking virgin?"

Which would have upset me sooooooo much at any other time, because I hate it when people think I'm this naive virgin. But for some reason, that's not how I reacted when you were holding me down and fucking me, telling me how tight my pussy was and asking me if I was a virgin. That's not how I reacted at all.

Instead, I came again.

I'd never had that experience. I mean, to just come like that, randomly, suddenly, not expecting it—it was wild. Totally wild. I would have done anything for you. So when you pulled out of me and grabbed my wrists and forced me up, into a sitting position, it's not like I was going to say "no"—the real "no" *or* the fake "no." I just wanted it, bad, and I knew what was coming.

Okay, I've never done it. I mean, now I have. But I'd never done it before last night. I didn't think I wanted to. And I mean, I *really* never thought I'd do it right after it pulled out of my pussy.

But I was yours. Totally, utterly. Without a will of my own except to get more of your cock—every way I could.

You said "Suck it!" with this sound that told me you said it to her all the time. I mean, I know she does it. A lot. She really loves it. She talks to me about it all the time. She even loves to swallow.

But it's not that I was afraid you would figure out I wasn't her. I was just....well, I wanted it. I wanted it bad.

So I just sort of *went* with it.

Your cock's really big. Really, really big. I mean, it doesn't even quite fit in my mouth, really. I have to open wide for it, really wide. But I did, open wide, and I just sort of started *sucking* it.

God, it was incredible. I could feel my pussy throb with each stroke I gave you down your thick shaft. I wanted it so bad, I wanted all of it.

I know she deep throats. I mean, she tells me everything. She even told me how to do it. I don't think she ever thought I'd be doing it to *you*, though.

But at that moment, I didn't care. I just wanted it in me, all the way.

So I took a deep breath. A really, really deep breath,

because your cock's really big. And as I felt the head, thick against the back of my throat, I swallowed.

Don't get me wrong, I was scared. You're huge. And I'd never done it before. Never sucked cock, I mean. And definitely never had anything down my throat. I mean, I was *beyond* scared. I just wanted it really, really bad. If I could have backed out, I would. But it's not that you wouldn't let me back out—all I had to do was say your name and you'd know who I was. It was that I couldn't bear the thought of not having your cock every possible place in my body that it would fit—even if it didn't, you know, really fit.

I counted. It took me like eight tries. I know it sometimes takes her two or three, so I felt my face reddening and I was afraid you'd know it wasn't her because it took me so long to get it down. But if you noticed the difference, you didn't say anything. Instead, you just put your head back and moaned.

God, it was a turn-on. Hearing you moan like that, and knowing I was doing it to you. If I'd had my vibrator on my clit I would have come. But of course, that was out of the question—she hates vibrators. Never uses them.

So I just reached down and touched my clit, and it happened again.

It was getting strange. I mean, I'd never come like this before, and I didn't even think girls *could* come from giving head. I mean, you know, that movie *Deep Throat* isn't real, is it? I don't fucking know, but the fullness of your cock down my throat just made me do it. It felt like there was a direct connection between your cock and my clit, and I only had to rub myself like three little, little strokes to make it happen.

Your hips pumped rhythmically and my face met each little thrust. Now it was easy; my throat felt wide open and I was totally into the rhythm of it. I didn't even think about how big your cock was in terms of not being able to take it....I thought about how turned on I was to be swallowing it, wanting it, needing it more than I'd ever needed anything. I could hear you moaning in that way guys do, you know, not that I have a lot of experience, but I've heard it before, and I know what it means. You were close. Really, really close. And I knew that maybe if I kept doing what I was doing you'd come, just come right in my mouth. Down my throat. That sent a fresh, intense, overwhelming surge of excitement through my body, and I wanted it. I wanted your come, even though I'd never tasted it before, even though I had no idea if I'd even be *able* to swallow. But I know she swallows, so I figured it'd be okay. And I wanted it so bad, I would have done anything to get it.

But you had other things in mind. You weren't finished with me yet.

You guided me around, onto my hands and knees. I know she loves it this way. I like it too. I mean, I haven't done it that much, but I knew I liked it. I fantasize about it a lot.

Your cock still seemed huge, though. It was harder for me to take it in this position. My pussy felt tighter, and your cock felt bigger. Maybe that's why I gasped, why I moaned so loud when I felt your cockhead against my pussy again.

But I wanted it. I really, really wanted it.

So I pushed back onto you, and you gave it to me fast, like I know she likes it. Like *I* like it, I guess. Like I wanted it, then, hard, merciless, driving into me so it almost hurt—almost, but not quite.

And you fucked me. You fucked me hard, fast, your hips pumping your cock into me as I fucked back onto you. God, I came so hard. I don't know how, I shouldn't have been coming. I mean, I'd already come three times....four? Maybe five. I don't know. But I came again. I came so hard and I just moaned and moaned, not even caring if you realized it was me. Not caring about anything but your cock, deep inside me, hitting my G-spot like I told you. Maybe that's why I came so hard. Maybe that's why I wanted you to come inside me so bad.

But you didn't. Not there, anyway. I felt your hand tracing a path down my back, over the bunched-up skirt, over the garter belt. I felt your thumb pressing against my hole.

I heard you chuckling, knowingly.

"You're ready for me," you said.

Your cock felt as big coming out as going in. It left this big void inside me, inside my pussy, a void I wanted filled.

"Please," I moaned softly. "Please....please...."

I guess I knew it was coming. I guess I wanted it. Yes, I definitely wanted it. I was a little scared—I mean, it had felt so good when I put that vibrator in my butt, just a little bit, but your cock is so, so big. I mean, really big.

But I didn't tell you to stop. I couldn't even summon a request for you to slow down. I know it was hard for her at first to take it that way, because you're so big. But now she takes it easy, and she likes it that way. And you love to give it to her.

So you didn't slow down. You didn't give it to me gently.

You pushed into me, and my eyes went wide in the darkness. Sensation flooded my body. My pulse pounded in my ears, and I felt my hole expanding, stretching—I thought it was going to hurt, and maybe it did, a little, just for a second. But then you were in me, and I couldn't believe it, but I was opening up for it. I was taking it that way—the way I thought I couldn't. The way *she* likes it, you know—the dirty way, I guess.

And god, it felt so incredible.

It felt so good I pushed back onto you. I felt you going deep into my ass, and you didn't give me a moment to catch my breath.

You started fucking me fast, hard, like you didn't care if

it felt good. But it did. It felt incredible. Remember what I told you about your cock and my G-spot? I know it's not possible, but it felt like your cock was hitting right there—almost like it was hitting my clit from the *inside*. I knew I was going to come.

And you were, too. I'm really tight back there, I guess, and maybe it just felt really good to you. But you weren't in there very long, maybe twenty strokes, thirty, I don't know. I heard you groaning and I knew you were going to come in my ass.

Which drove me right over the edge, into the most intense orgasm of all. I came so hard I think I bit my lip. It still feels raw. I think I actually started crying, it felt so good. I grabbed at the pillows and threw them across the room. I pushed my hands against the wall and shoved myself onto you. I felt you pumping and heard your moans and knew you were coming inside me, somewhere no come had ever been.

It seemed like you came for a really long time. When your cock slid out, I felt so incredibly wet in there. My legs were weak and I was shaking. You slumped down on the bed next to me and I writhed there, not believing the sensations that were going through my body.

It was like I was in a trance. I stripped off my clothes, wriggling around on the bed, just because I wanted to feel my naked body against yours. You stayed still, breathing heavily, while I rubbed my body all over you. You were moist with sweat. I licked it off your chest and the salty taste made me so hungry for you I could feel my pussy hurting, wanting your cock, still, despite how good you'd given it to me. I felt really sad, like I wished I could have it every night for the rest of my life, have your cock inside me. But I knew I couldn't, so I decided to just love you while I could. What the hell, right? It's not like you were complaining.

I snuggled up against you, feeling your naked body against mine and I listened to you sleep.

So that's what I remember, that's what I think happened. If you don't remember it, maybe something's a little different. But one thing I know—we should never do it again. Never.

I didn't sleep at all, just sprawled there with my face against your chest, smelling you, not even able to smell her any more. I just felt your chest rise and fall as you slept, felt the softness of your cock, slick and savory, in my hand as I cradled it, remembering what it felt like inside me. I felt my heart pound and thought and thought and thought about what I was going to say when you woke up.

And so I guess this is what I said, to tell you the story and let you know why it happened. To answer the question on your face when you looked into my eyes, to answer the many questions, and maybe hope that you would tell me your side of it, so I would understand why in all those questions I saw in your eyes there wasn't the faintest hint of anger, or regret, or even, I guess, really, guilt.

I mean, I don't know that. I still don't know why you looked at me so naturally, why you looked at me and smiled—surprised, sure. But pleased, maybe, satisfied, even? I don't know—relieved? It was kind of weird. You looked like you were glad to see me. And instead of saying "What the fuck are you doing here with my come in your ass," you just smiled, stroked my hair, and said my name. You said good morning, and you said my name.

You've got to admit that was pretty weird.

It was an accident. And we should never, ever do it again.

What are you doing? Oh, wow. You shouldn't. Yes, that feels good, sure, but....no. Don't do that. No, really. I'm serious. Safeword safeword safeword.

Oh, wow.

About the Authors

Thomas Roche is a worker-owner at San Francisco's Good Vibrations and the author of more than 150 published short stories that have appeared in such publications as the *Best American Erotica* series, the *Mammoth Book of Erotica* series, and many other anthologies, magazines and websites. His web projects have included work on Good Vibes Magazine (www.goodvibes.com), Universal Studios' 13th Street (13thstreet.com), and Gothic Net (www.gothic.net). Books he has edited include three volumes of the *Noirotica* series of erotic crime-noir and the soon-to-be-released *Best Men's Erotica* (Cleis). His own short story collections include *Dark Matter* and two collaborations with Alison Tyler, *His* and *Hers*.

Alison Tyler is a shy girl with a dirty mind. She is the author of more than 15 sexy novels including *Learning to Love It, Strictly Confidential, Sweet Thing,* and *Sticky Fingers* (all published by Black Lace) and *The ESP Affair* and *Blue Valentine* (published by Magic Carpet Books). Her short stories have appeared in anthologies including *Sweet Life, Erotic Travel Tales I & II, Best Women's Erotica 2002 & 2003, Best Fetish Erotica,* and *Best Lesbian Erotica 1996* (all published by Cleis), as well as *Wicked Words 4, 5 & 6* (Black Lace). She was a runner-up in *Penthouse Variations'* Baudelaire Fiction Contest. Ms. Tyler lives with her partner of seven years in the San Francisco Bay Area—but she misses L.A.

Pretty Things Press

Naughty Stories From A to Z

Bondage on a Budget

Naughty Stories From A to Z—Volume 2

30 Erotic Tales Written Just For Him

30 Erotic Tales Written Just For Her

Bad Girl

www.prettythingspress.com